Stolen Kisses, Secrets, and Lies

Mob Princess

For Money and Love
Count Your Blessings

Also by Todd Strasser

Shirt and Shoes Not Required
Boot Camp
Can't Get There from Here
Give a Boy a Gun
The Drift X series
The Impact Zone series

MOB
Princess
Stolen Kisses, Secrets, and Lies

Todd Strasser

Simon Pulse
NEW YORK   LONDON   TORONTO   SYDNEY

This book is a work of fiction. Any references to historical events, real people, or real locales are used fictitiously. Other names, characters, places, and incidents are the product of the author's imagination, and any resemblance to actual events or locales or persons, living or dead, is entirely coincidental.

SIMON PULSE
An imprint of Simon & Schuster Children's Publishing Division
1230 Avenue of the Americas, New York, NY 10020
Copyright © 2007 by Todd Strasser
All rights reserved, including the right of reproduction
in whole or in part in any form.
SIMON PULSE and colophon are registered trademarks of
Simon & Schuster, Inc.
Designed by Mike Rosamilia
The text of this book was set in New Caledonia.
Manufactured in the United States of America
First Simon Pulse edition September 2007
2 4 6 8 10 9 7 5 3 1
Library of Congress Control Number 2007930642
ISBN-13: 978-1-4169-3541-4
ISBN-10: 1-4169-3541-X

TO MY CREW, LIA AND GEOFF

Thanks to Bethany and Jen for giving me the green light,
and for helping me get there.

Part 1
Winter

"**DAD KNOWS I SPENT LAST NIGHT WITH NICK BLATTARIA.**" A tear rolled down Kate Blessing's cheek. She was sitting with her mother at a table in the back of a Riverton Starbucks. At almost every table around her someone was sitting alone with a laptop.

Her mother, Amanda, blinked with astonishment. "Joe Blattaria's son?"

Kate nodded miserably. It was a cold, gray Saturday morning in January. Outside, people passed, bundled in coats, hats, and scarves. Half an hour ago her father had banned her from their house. Bleary from lack of sleep, Kate had driven to her mother's new apartment in the River House, the fanciest building in Riverton.

"I don't understand," Amanda Blessing said, hooking her blond hair behind her ear. She looked understandably bewildered, since Joe Blattaria was her husband's sworn enemy. "What were you doing with Nick Blattaria?"

Kate explained that she'd gone to Atlantic City the night before with Nick to find out how strong the Blattaria organization was.

"Your father agreed to that?" Amanda asked, eyes wide with disbelief.

"It was supposed to be a fact-finding mission, that's all," Kate explained, dabbing her cheek dry with a paper napkin. "Mom, try to understand. Ever since you moved out, Dad's been a mess. The house is a filthy wreck. Uncle Benny's trying to take over the organization from the inside, and the Blattarias are moving in on our territory. Dad would never admit that he's desperate, but I think he is. I thought finding out more about the Blattarias would help."

"I understand," Amanda said. "But I still can't believe he'd let you go to Atlantic City with the son of his worst enemy."

"I thought I could manage the situation," Kate said. "In the last few weeks I've handled the guys in Dad's organization really well. At least twice I've stopped Uncle Benny from taking over. I've come up with good ideas and solutions to problems. Dad's been really impressed. So when I told him Nick was interested in me, it made—"

"What!?" Amanda interrupted. "How did Nick get *interested* in you? How did he even get to *know* you?"

Kate explained how Franky Big Bones and Nick had come to the house to talk about the Brinks robbery.

Again Kate's mother stared at her in disbelief. "Your father let two members of the Blattaria organization into *our* home? My God, he really must be out of his mind."

Kate nodded.

"So that's how you met Nick?" Amanda assumed.

"Right," said Kate. "And right away I could tell he was interested in me. Anyway, one of Dad's problems is that the Blattarias keep threatening us, but we don't know if they're really strong enough to do anything about it, or just bluffing."

"So you went to Atlantic City with Nick last night to find out," Amanda said.

Kate nodded and ran her fingers through her long black hair. She felt weary. She needed to sleep, she needed to shower, she needed to fix her hair, she needed to *think*.

"And what did you find out?" her mother asked.

Kate's eyes got watery again as the memory returned of the previous night with Nick in that fabulous Atlantic City hotel casino. "I really like him, Mom. He's good-looking and sweet and considerate and funny. And last night was just so . . ." Kate wasn't sure what word to use.

Her mother gave her a bittersweet smile. "Wonderful?"

Kate felt wretched. Tears ran down her cheeks, and she dabbed them away. A guy with a beard at the next table looked up from his laptop and stared at her. Kate hated crying in public. Earlier she'd wanted to go up to her mom's apartment where they could be alone. But when she'd called up from the lobby, her mom had told her to wait until she could come down and they'd go out for coffee.

"And now you're miserable because your father's banned you from the house, and you've come to your senses and realized that

5

regardless of how fabulous Nick Blattaria is, he's the last guy in the world you ever should have become intimate with." Amanda Blessing had a gift for summation.

Kate nodded and started to cry harder. The guy with the beard stared again. Kate's mom, who looked like Michelle Pfeiffer, glared at him. "Mind your own business," she snapped. The guy quickly looked down at his computer, and Amanda slid around the table next to Kate. "It's all right." She put her arm around her daughter's shoulders and hugged her. "These things happen. Haven't you ever heard of 'sleeping with the enemy'?"

"He doesn't *have* to be the enemy," Kate said with a sniff.

"He does as long as Joe Blattaria is alive and breathing," Amanda said.

"But it's so stupid," Kate said. "Instead of fighting each other, why can't our organizations join forces? I mean, think of the synergy."

Amanda laughed.

"I'm serious," Kate insisted, frustrated.

Her mother reached over and gave her a hug. "I know you are, and I'm sorry I laughed. You realize, there isn't a man in *either* organization that knows what that word means?"

"Nick does," Kate said.

"Nick's a long way from having any real say in what happens in his father's organization," Amanda said.

"He's in charge of their Atlantic City and Las Vegas operations," said Kate. "He flew to Vegas this morning."

Amanda's eyes widened slightly. "The Blattarias have Atlantic City and Las Vegas operations?"

"Yes," Kate said. "While Dad's always been happy just doing business in Riverton, the Blattarias have been expanding. They understand business theory. You have to grow to survive."

"I guess greed sounds better when it's called business theory," her mother mused.

"It's not greed, Mom," Kate said, applying what she'd learning in the Future Business Leaders of America. "It's the nature of capitalist markets."

"I know, hon. I was just trying to be clever," Amanda said.

Kate took a sip of her cappuccino. The milk steamer behind the coffee bar hissed. At a table near theirs two women laughed loudly. Kate's heart ached. "What should I do about Nick?"

"Maybe we should wait to talk about that," her mother said.

"What's the point, Mom?" Kate asked. "You're going to tell me I can't see Nick again and I have to patch things up with Dad, right?"

Amanda nodded. "I don't think you have a choice, hon."

Kate's heart sank to new depths. Deep inside, she knew that was the only real answer. Still, hearing her mother confirm it only made her feel worse. "But I *really* like him. I mean, he's the first guy I've ever felt this way about. It's not fair."

Amanda sipped her espresso and was quiet for a moment. Then she said, "I know this might sound like a strange question, but is there . . . anyone else?"

"You mean, another guy?" Kate asked as if that was the last

thing on her mind. But even as she said it, the handsome blond image of rich, charming Teddy Fitzgerald flashed into her head.

"It doesn't have to be someone serious," her mother said. "Just someone to help get your mind off Nick."

If anyone could do that, it was Teddy. Kate liked him. She was *fond* of him. But he didn't conjure up the whirlwind of emotions she felt when she thought about Nick.

"Sometimes slow and steady is better than fast and furious," Amanda counseled.

"But *you* went for fast and furious," Kate said.

"Right," said her mother. "And look where it got me."

"But it was your choice to leave," Kate said. "Dad didn't want you to go."

"Sometimes the other person doesn't have to make you go," Amanda said. "All they have to do is make it impossible for you to stay."

Kate understood. Throughout her parents' marriage her father had been a serial bimbo chaser, and that had been hard on her mom. But the recent news that her father had gotten his latest bimbo pregnant was the deal breaker. Anyone could understand why her mother had finally had enough and left.

"Are you sure I can't convince you to come home?" Kate asked. "The house is falling apart without you."

"You're not trying to guilt trip me, are you?" her mother asked.

"I'm just telling you how it is," Kate said, and yawned.

"We're not talking about me," Amanda said. "We're talking about you. And right now you need to get some sleep."

Her mom was right. Kate had been up almost all night with Nick. She was exhausted.

"Let's go back to the apartment," Amanda said.

They went back to the River House, a new red-brick high-rise with green-tinted windows. Kate's mom made her wait outside in the red carpeted hallway while she went into the apartment and straightened up. Kate protested that she didn't care if the place was messy, but her mother insisted. Finally, she let Kate in. The apartment was large, sunny, modern, and practically bare. There were no rugs on the dark wood floors and no paintings on the white walls.

"I've only had time to buy a kitchen table, some chairs, a couch, a television, and a bed," Amanda explained.

"It's really nice, Mom," Kate said, although she was dismayed by the furniture purchases. They were quality pieces—the black leather couch, the flat-screen HDTV—things that implied that her mother wasn't planning on coming home anytime soon.

Amanda gestured toward the bedroom. "Why don't you go lie down?"

"Thanks, Mom." Kate yawned again. She went into the bedroom—empty and bare except for a reading lamp and queen-size bed—and did just that.

When Kate opened her eyes, it was starting to get dark out. For a moment she was disoriented, until she remembered she was in her mother's apartment and it was early January and the sun set before five p.m.

Kate switched on the light next to the bed and sat up. The bedroom door was open and the rest of the apartment was dark. "Mom?"

There was no answer. Kate got out of the bed and went into the bathroom to wash. A *Golf Digest* magazine lay on the window sill. Since when had her mom started reading that? Was she planning on taking up golf in her newfound free time? Leaving the bedroom, Kate turned on the light in the hall and found a note on a table next to the door.

> **K—Went to meet a friend. Hope you're feeling better. Had a long talk with your father. You can go home. He's not angry anymore. Love, Mom**

Wow, Kate thought. *Good work, Mom.* Feeling relieved, she put on her coat and left the apartment. Outside, the streetlights were on and the sky was a thick layer of dark clouds. To Kate it smelled like snow was coming.

Despite her mom's note, when Kate got home she still felt nervous. Standing in the high-ceilinged black marble foyer, she could hear, coming from upstairs, loud grunts followed by the clank of metal, and then a jarring thud as if something heavy had been dropped. It was her brother, Sonny Jr., lifting weights. A peculiar smell wafted into Kate's nose. It took a moment to realize that it was rotting garbage.

Doesn't anyone besides me know how to throw out the garbage? Kate wondered as she headed for the kitchen.

Unfortunately, the closer she got, the stronger the odor grew. The kitchen was a mess—the green marble counter covered with dirty plates and take-out containers, the double sinks overflowing with pots and plates.

"For God's sake," Kate muttered to herself as she tied the smelly garbage bag closed and started to pull it out of the can.

"Kate?" The sound of her father's voice made her jump.

Kate spun around and saw him sitting in the shadows in the darkened family room. "Dad? Why don't you turn on a light?"

Sonny Blessing didn't answer.

"I'm just going to get rid of this garbage," Kate said, and headed out of the kitchen. Outside, small white snow flakes had begun to drift out of the dark sky. She left the garbage bag outside the front door, making a mental note to take it down to the curb the next time she went out.

When she returned to the kitchen, her father was still sitting in the family room. Kate sat opposite him. Even in the dim light she could see that dark stubble blanketed her father's jaw and his hair was unkempt. His normally neatly pressed clothes were wrinkled and looked slept in.

"I'm sorry, Dad," she said. "I made a mistake."

"I spoke to your mom," Sonny said. "Know what she said? That this is payback."

"What do you mean?"

"She was talking about all the women I've charmed and seduced over the years," Sonny said.

Kate understood, but her father's answer felt like the stab of a very sharp knife. "So when your own daughter gets charmed and seduced it's payback?"

Sonny slowly nodded. "What goes around, comes around, you know?"

Kate felt an ache in her heart. It wasn't that way with her and Nick. She wasn't just some bimbo he'd used and discarded. But she wasn't about to explain to her father that the seduction had been mutual. Her father may have used all those women, but Kate didn't feel used. Not by Nick. She was certain his attraction to her was sincere.

"So you promise you'll never, ever see that punk kid again," Sonny said. It was a command, not a request. Kate felt a deep, painful ache in her heart. It was so unfair. And yet, for now, and for the sake of her family, she said, "Yes."

2

I T SNOWED ALL WEEKEND. KATE STAYED IN AND CAUGHT up on her sleep and studies and did some housecleaning. But she couldn't get Nick out of her head. Maybe she'd promised never to see him again, but did that mean they couldn't talk? Mostly she just wanted him to call. She wanted to hear his voice and know that Friday night had been special for him, too.

But the weekend passed and her cell phone didn't ring. She told herself that he was probably busy in Vegas, but not hearing from him hurt just the same.

On Monday morning before school Kate went down to the kitchen to make coffee. Once again, it was a mess. On Saturday night, unable to sleep thanks to her late afternoon nap, she had straightened and cleaned. Now it was barely thirty-six hours later and she was pushing dirty plates out of the way to find a place on the counter for her coffee mug.

Sonny Jr. came into the kitchen wearing a sleeveless black muscle shirt. Her brother was thirteen, short, and chubby.

Recently he'd started lifting weights, but to Kate the muscle shirt looked a little premature. His arms were pink and shapeless.

Sonny Jr. got a bowl and a box of Honey Nut Cheerios from a cupboard. At the kitchen counter he used his forearm to sweep junk out of the way. In the process an empty take-out container fell to the floor. Ignoring it, Kate's brother headed for the refrigerator for the milk. He was pouring it into the bowl of cereal when he noticed the look on Kate's face.

"What?" he said in a preemptively annoyed tone.

"You knocked a take-out container on the floor and just left it there," Kate said.

"So?"

"So who's going to pick it up?" Kate asked.

Her brother shrugged and scooped a spoonful of cereal into his mouth.

"I spent all of Saturday night cleaning up this kitchen and now it's a pigsty again," Kate said. "Would it kill you to make half an effort to keep it neat?"

Sonny Jr. chewed loudly, making a crunching sound like boots stomping through dry leaves and twigs. He rolled his eyes in a way that said, *Get real.*

"And it's freezing outside," Kate said. "Don't you think you'll be cold in that shirt?"

Her brother chewed and didn't answer.

"I don't know what you think you're showing off, anyway," Kate added.

Sonny Jr. swallowed. "You're just mad because of that guy."

Caught by surprise, Kate forced a derisive laugh. "What?"

"Don't pretend you don't know," her brother said. "Of all the guys in the world, you had to pick the son of Dad's worst enemy. How lame is that?"

Kate opened her mouth to retaliate, but no words came out. No doubt her brother had overheard something. Sonny Jr.'s question drained the fight out of her. He was right. So right. *What had she been thinking?* How could someone who prided herself on being so level-headed, so sensible, and so logical do something so ridiculous?

Kate felt tears welling up. *Not again!* Talk about ridiculous. When had she ever cried this much over a guy? Not wanting Sonny Jr. to see, she left the kitchen and went back upstairs, where she sat on the edge of her bed and sobbed wretchedly for ten minutes. When she was finished, she washed her face, reapplied her makeup, and went back downstairs. By then Sonny Jr. had left to catch the bus to the middle school. Kate pulled on her warm coat and went out the front door.

Outside there was a flash of black against the white snow as a flock of crows took flight. Kate instantly saw why. The snow-covered circle in front of the house was covered with garbage and shreds of torn black plastic. Kate groaned inwardly as she remembered that she'd put that smelly garbage bag outside on Saturday night, and then forgotten about it. The raccoons must have gotten into it first, and now the crows were picking through the crumbs. As if she wasn't already depressed enough, the sight of the dirty take-out containers, gnawed sparerib bones, pizza crusts, and other refuse scattered over the white snow bummed her out even more. Everything was going wrong.

She got into her car and drove to school. It was Monday and she had two video conferences to set up. One for the FBLA and the other for her father and the Blattarias. And that presented yet another problem: She'd have to see Teddy. Kate felt a pang of guilt. Before her fling with Nick in Atlantic City on Friday night, it might have appeared to the casual observer that she and Teddy had been moving gradually closer and closer. First, working together on the FBLA. Next, a kiss on New Year's Eve. And then their SAT dinner date just this past Friday before she went to AC with Nick.

Kate was still amazed at how much had happened in the past sixty hours. The night with Nick, then being banned from her house by her father and then taken back. But spending the night with Nick had other ramifications as well. She'd experienced a level of romance and emotion she'd never imagined before. Certainly nothing that she could conceive of sharing with Teddy, who was probably too young to be called stodgy but sort of fit the description anyway.

The thought of seeing Teddy here at school filled her with regret and dread. Even though they'd barely started going out, she still felt as if she'd cheated on him with Nick. As the end of sixth period approached, Kate felt more and more ill at ease. She and Teddy regularly met during seventh period to work on FBLA matters. And with the video conference that afternoon, there was no way she could avoid him.

Kate's heart drummed as she walked down the hall to the

school's TV studio. The door had a window, and she stopped to look in. Teddy was inside, moving chairs around. He had the blond good looks of a Lacoste model, and an intensity and sense of purpose that few guys his age possessed. She always smiled when she saw what he was wearing. Today it was a classic pair of LL Bean storm chasers, navy blue wide-wale corduroys, and a light blue oxford shirt with a frayed collar under a yellow cable-knit sweater with a hole at the right elbow. The effect was sort of scruffy old-money prep, and the reason Teddy got away with it was that there was plenty of old money in his family.

Trying to calm her nerves, Kate took a deep breath and let it out slowly, then opened the door and went in. Jazz was playing on the sound system. Teddy turned and smiled. Kate had hoped that he'd stay on the other side of the room, but he came toward her. Kate froze and inwardly prayed that he would stop short, but he moved close, probably for a hello kiss. She offered him her cheek.

Teddy planted the kiss quickly, then backed away with a slight scowl on his face as if he was disappointed she hadn't offered her lips, even briefly. "How are you feeling?"

For a second Kate didn't understand why he'd asked. Then she remembered the excuse she'd given for cutting their dinner date short on Friday night.

"Oh, much better, thanks," she quickly said. But it was too late. Teddy knew she'd forgotten. He pursed his lips and averted his eyes. Kate wondered if he was merely disappointed because he'd caught her in a lie. Or was it a deeper disappointment because he liked her and she'd blown him off?

Either one made her feel awful. Teddy had only been good to her. And while right now the guy she really wanted was Nick— whom she could never have—she knew the time might come when she'd feel differently. So she said, "But I'd love to go out again some time." And then, despite the fact that she'd enjoyed eating Big Willy's Hubba-Hubba chili cheese dogs and fries, she added, "But next time maybe someplace where the food's a little easier on the digestive system."

Now Teddy's smile was authentic. "I'm sure that can be arranged."

Kate felt both better and worse. Better because she'd just repaired whatever damage she'd done by forgetting that she'd pretended to feel ill on Friday night. But worse because no matter what her mother said about finding someone to help her get her mind off Nick, she didn't want to lead Teddy on. He was too nice for that.

Together they started preparing for the video conference, moving tables and chairs, setting up the video cameras and microphones, and making sure all the equipment worked. Their deal with the school's TV studio techies was that the FBLA could do what they wanted in the studio as long as they left it in the condition they'd found it in. Kate and Teddy had just finished setting up when the bell rang. Teddy turned off the jazz. It was time to go to their next classes.

They headed for the door at the same time. Suddenly Kate realized that they'd be uncomfortably close if they went through the doorway together. But Teddy, ever the gentleman, stopped and gestured for her to go through first. Kate wondered if he'd done it out of natural politeness, or because he didn't want to put her in the awkward position of being close enough for a good-bye kiss. Either way, she appreciated the gesture.

As soon as school ended, Kate hurried back to the TV studio for the video conference with Middletown High. While she did care about the FBLA, her main concern was making sure that the system worked for the second conference later that night. As far as ensuring that certain doors would be left open later, that had been easy to arrange. Kate had handed over two of the hundred-dollar bills from her Friday night casino winnings to a friendly janitor, and in return had received assurances that everything would be taken care of.

Three hours later the video-conferenced joint chapter event with the Middletown branch of the FBLA was over. The two schools had competed on business calculations, impromptu speaking, and mock job interviews, and had ended with a business ethics debate. The whole thing had been recorded on CD for the state competition so that it would count as a multimedia project as well. Kate congratulated her fellow members of the Riverton High FBLA as they filed out of the studio, smiling, happy, but mostly tired and eager to get home for dinner. It wasn't long before only Kate and Teddy were left in the studio. She was hungry, but hoped he wouldn't ask her to have dinner. She felt too mixed up to know what to do or say.

"What did you think?" Teddy asked.

"I thought we did well," Kate said, pulling a CD out of her

laptop. "And we've got the whole thing on CD for the scrapbook."

Teddy gave her the thumbs-up sign, then looked at his watch. "I promised Dad I'd meet him for dinner," he said, and gestured at the array of tables and chairs, the empty candy wrappers and crumbled scrap paper on the floor, "but I hate leaving you to clean up."

"It's no problem," Kate said. The truth was, she had a couple of hours to kill before the next video conference—the one Teddy didn't know about.

"No, Blessing, seriously," Teddy said. "I don't want you to do this alone. Suppose we come in early tomorrow morning and straighten up?"

It had been a long day, and it wasn't over. Kate decided not to argue. "Okay."

Teddy picked up his coat. "Great. See you then." He went to the door and held it open, apparently expecting her to leave school with him. Unable to think of an excuse to stay behind, she got her coat. At this time of night the halls were empty. Their footsteps echoed on the tile floors.

They stepped out into the chilly night air and headed for the senior parking lot. Kate could tell Teddy had something on his mind and she feared it was going to be serious, about the two of them. If ever there were a moment in her life when she wasn't prepared to deal with that, it was right now. Teddy walked her to her car. Their breaths were plumes of white vapor in the dark.

"Kate?" he said.

She stopped. She couldn't remember the last time he'd called her by her first name. Now she was certain something serious was coming. She held her breath.

"You know I . . . I really enjoy working with you," Teddy said. "I don't mean for this to sound sexist, but for a female you really have an incredibly logical mind. If you do decide to go into business someday, I think you'll be a tremendous success."

This wasn't at all what she'd expected. Caught by surprise, Kate was relieved and pleased. She was relieved that he hadn't brought up anything too emotional. And she was genuinely pleased that he thought so highly of her. Coming from Teddy Fitzgerald's lips, the compliment really meant something. Considering his family, Teddy probably knew more about business than almost anyone else in school, teachers included.

But the good feeling was quickly replaced by a bad one: Yet another day was almost over and she still hadn't heard from Nick.

Teddy must have seen the change in her expression. "I only meant it as a compliment," he quickly added.

Kate felt a crooked smile grow on her lips. There was no way he could have known that she was thinking about Nick. She felt a twinge of regret. Not because she'd gone with Nick instead of Teddy. But that she'd gone with Nick at all.

"I know you meant it as a compliment, Teddy. I'm sorry if I seem distracted. There's just some confusing things going on in my life right now."

"Anything I can help you with?" Teddy quickly volunteered.

The smile on Kate's lips became more genuine. Teddy was so sweet, and willing, and sincere. She stepped closer and gave him a quick hug. "You're the best, Teddy. Really, I don't know what I'd do without you."

She got in her car and drove out of the lot as if she were heading home, but at the next intersection she turned right instead of left. As she drove through the dark she wasn't sure where she was going, but she had time before her father and his associates arrived for the video conference with the Blattarias. She could have driven aimlessly, her direction as uncertain as her feelings, but she was hungry.

The diner was crowded and busy. The counter was jammed and most of the booths were full. Kate spotted an empty booth in the back and started toward it. Two people were sitting in the booth next to the empty one, their heads tilted toward each other as if they were whispering. Lovers on the sly, sharing sweet nothings, Kate thought wistfully, wishing her own love life could be so simple and free. But as she sat down she noticed a familiar and expensive-looking chocolate-brown shearling coat hanging on a hook. Kate glanced into the wall mirror and had a shock. Her best friend Randi was staring back at her with a startled look on her face.

Kate focused on the guy sitting across from Randi. He had short blond hair and looked older. It was that cute new English teacher, Mr. Brenner. Seeing Kate in the mirror, he forced a smile onto his lips and nodded as if to say hi. But talk about an awkward situation!

"Uh, hey, Randi." Kate tried to pretend there was nothing unusual about finding a teacher and student whispering in a booth in the back of the diner.

"Hi, Kate," Randi said. "You know Mr. Brenner, right?"

"Sure." Standing in the aisle, Kate gave him a little wave. On the table between Randi and the teacher was a half-finished omelet and the remains of a deluxe burger plate with fries.

"Want to join us?" Randi asked. Kate couldn't tell whether the offer was sincere or just a matter of expedience—Randi's way of trying to show that everything was innocent.

"Oh, no, that's okay, thanks," she said. "I'm sure you guys have lots to talk about."

"Don't be silly, join us," Mr. Brenner said.

Kate glanced at Randi, who nodded back as if it was okay.

"Thanks," Kate said, and sat down next to her friend. Randi had brushed out her dark hair and was wearing a tight, low-cut top, providing Mr. Brenner a revealing view of her ample cleavage.

"We're just hanging out until the audition begins," Randi said, clearly feeling the need to explain what she was doing there with a teacher.

Kate was lost for a moment. "Auditions?"

"For the community theater," Randi said. "*Guys and Dolls*, remember?"

"Oh, right," Kate said. "So how's it look? Think enough people will try out?" In the past Randi had sometimes complained that it was difficult to find enough actors for some of the plays she'd been in.

"We were just talking about that," Randi said. "Derek— I mean, Mr. Brenner—is worried that he picked the wrong play."

"It's a guy-heavy musical," Mr. Brenner explained. "And that can be iffy for community theater."

"Couldn't you have some of the women dress up like men?" Kate asked.

"Wouldn't that be cool?" Randi gasped excitedly and turned to Mr. Brenner. "We could do it campy. It would be awesome."

Mr. Brenner didn't share her excitement. "That might work for high school. But the community theater audience? I don't think we want to go there."

Now Kate remembered that Randi was codirecting the play. Somehow that made it more understandable that the two of them would be having dinner together. She still wasn't sure what to think about the whispering.

"How's codirecting?" she asked.

"I am so amped," Randi said. "Derek says I have great energy. I just need to be reined in now and then."

The waitress came and Kate ordered a Cobb salad. Mr. Brenner's cell phone rang. He slid out of the booth and took the call outside.

"His wife?" Kate asked in a low voice.

Randi shook her head. "I don't think so."

"Girlfriend?" Kate asked.

Randi shrugged. "Who knows?"

"But you hope not, right?" Kate guessed.

Randi gave her a sly grin.

"Randi, he's a *teacher*," Kate hissed.

"So?"

"He could lose his job."

Randi waved the idea away. "Not likely. I mean, if it ever went that far, which it probably won't."

"Could we change 'probably' to 'definitely'?" Kate asked.

Randi rolled her eyes. "You are so last century."

"Not anymore." The words sprang from Kate's lips as if they had a mind of their own. She'd been determined not to say anything about Nick and Friday night.

Randi gave her a curious look. "You're *not* so last century?"

The urge to tell her best friend was greater than Kate had expected. She gave Randi a half smile, half shrug, as if to say, *My bad.*

Randi's eyes widened. *"Really!?"*

"Shh." Kate pressed a finger to her lips.

"With Teddy?"

The question caught Kate off guard, and before she could recover, Randi had divined the truth. *"Omigod!* It was someone else!"

"Keep it down!" Kate whispered. "And so help me, if you ever breathe a word to anyone . . ."

"Save your breath," Randi said. "Remember the Brinks truck? If you haven't figured out by now that your secrets are safe with me . . ."

She was right. "Sorry," Kate apologized.

"So who was the lucky stud?" Randi asked.

Kate shook her head. "I can't."

"Oh, come on," Randi said. "Don't I tell you everything?"

"This goes *beyond* 'everything'."

"Beyond everything?" Randi repeated, and mulled it over. "He's married?"

"No!"

"In a really committed, serious relationship?"

"Stop," Kate said. "Please? I can't tell you and I can't tell you why I can't tell you. I've already told you more than I should have."

Randi sat back, crossed her arms, and stuck out her lower lip in a pout. "Some friend."

"If you're really my friend, you'll cease and desist," Kate said.

Randi relented. "Oh, okay. But you're no fun."

"I thought you'd be congratulating me," Kate said.

"True that. Congratulations. Was it nice?"

"Yes," Kate said. "Very nice. I took your advice."

Randi looked vacant for a moment, then remembered. "Oh, you mean about hooking up with someone who has experience? Smart girl."

The waiter brought Kate's Cobb salad and she began to pick at it. She suddenly had less appetite than she'd thought. There was something else she needed to speak to Randi about, but she wasn't sure this was the right time or place.

"So what are you doing here, anyway?" Randi asked.

"Nothing much to eat at home," Kate said. That was at least half true.

"What's the latest with your mom?" Randi asked.

"I saw her new place."

"Guess she's not planning on coming home anytime soon, huh?" Randi said.

"Guess not," Kate said glumly.

Mr. Brenner returned. "We should probably get back to school. Almost time for the auditions."

Randi got up. "Talk to you later?"

Kate nodded.

"And congratulations," Randi said with a wink.

3

A LITTLE WHILE LATER KATE LEFT HER HALF-EATEN salad and returned to school. It was close to eight p.m. and the building was dark, except for the lights near the auditorium where the auditions for the community theater were being held. As promised, certain doors had been left open and Kate was able to enter unnoticed. Her father arrived at the TV studio just a moment after she did. Kate was shocked at how gaunt and tired he looked. His clothes were wrinkled and he carried several days' worth of dark stubble on his jaw.

"You okay?" she asked.

Sonny shrugged indifferently. "What's okay?"

Not an encouraging answer. "Dad, I hate to see you like this," Kate said. "If you're still upset about me and Nick . . ."

Her father averted his eyes. "It's not that. It's just not an easy time." Given what Kate knew, this sounded like an understatement. Her father looked as if he were carrying the weight of the world on his shoulders.

"I know," Kate said. "By the way, I did go to Atlantic City for a reason."

Sonny looked up at her with bloodshot eyes as if he'd forgotten. "So what did you find out?"

"The Blattarias have business in AC and Vegas. Nick flew out to Vegas Saturday morning. Either they're a strong, well-financed organization, or they're pulling off one of the greatest cons in history."

Sonny hung his head. "You think I blew it, kid?"

"No, I think you did what you believed was best for everyone," Kate said.

Her father nodded slowly. "I thought the knock-off merchandise and Internet scams were the best thing that ever happened to us. No more armed robberies. No more guys getting shot. I thought it would just go on forever. A nice, steady stream of income for everyone. Maybe not torrents of money, but enough so we could all be comfortable."

Kate couldn't bear to tell him that his business plan defied basic economic theory. Companies had to grow to remain healthy. Those that stagnated would either be squeezed out of the market by bigger, stronger companies or simply gobbled up by them.

"Our guys are losing faith," her father said. "Benny's goin' behind my back. If I had your mother to talk to, things might be different, but without her, it's a mess."

"Why can't you tell her that, Dad?" Kate asked. "What happened with the Tiffany situation, anyway?" Kate's mother had left her father after Tiffany, her father's most recent bimbo, had gotten pregnant.

"Nothing," Sonny said. "It was a scam."

"What do you mean?" Kate asked.

"She wanted money," Sonny said. "She thought if she said she was pregnant I'd give her some."

What kind of person would do that? Kate wondered with a shiver. "Can't you tell mom that? Tell her Tiffany means nothing to you. Promise you'll never mess around again, and buy her a fabulous mink coat. It's cold out and she'll really like that."

Sonny shook his head. "Not this time, kid."

"Why not?" Kate asked.

Instead of answering, her father glanced around the studio. "So how's this gonna work?"

Kate explained where her father and his guys would sit and which camera and monitor they'd face.

"And the Blattarias got the same setup over in Middletown?" Sonny asked.

"Exactly, Dad," Kate said. "It'll be almost as if you're in the same room with them."

The door opened and Willy Shoes came in wearing a brown plaid sports blazer over a green shirt and a black tie. His black leather shoes were polished to the point where they nearly glowed.

"Am I late?" he asked, even though the room was empty except for Sonny and Kate. Willy looked around and frowned. "Where is everyone?"

"They'll be here," said Sonny.

"What about the cameraman and the sound and the lighting?" Willy asked.

"It's all right here." Kate patted the video camera.

Willy made a face. "That's it? I thought we was gonna be on TV."

"You will," said Kate. "Through this camera."

"But who's gonna see me?" Willy asked.

"The Blattarias," said Sonny.

"That's all?" Willy said, clearly disappointed.

"Why don't you sit here?" Kate pointed to the chair right in front of the camera. "That way you'll be on center stage."

"Hey, all right." Willy seemed pleased that he would have a good seat.

Leo Sweets came in next with a bulge in his cheek and a half-eaten Snickers bar in his hand. Of all the guys in her father's organization, Leo was Kate's favorite. He was sweet and smart and understanding, like a doting grandfather. But Kate was dismayed to see his broad belly pushing against his old, stained tan tracksuit. Leo's weakness was sweets—candy and ice cream. Kate kept trying to get him to exercise and eat healthy, but every time she saw him he looked heavier than the time before.

"Hey!" With a broad smile—and missing only two teeth—Leo gathered Kate in his arms and gave her a big hug. "How's my sweetheart?"

"I'm good, Leo. You?"

"Couldn't be better," Leo Sweets said.

"Getting to the gym much?" Kate asked. The answer was obviously no, but she just wanted to remind him.

"You read my mind," Leo said. "That was my New Year's resolution."

"Really?" Kate said. "You've started going to the gym?"

"Any day now," Leo said. "I just gotta clear up my calendar and take care of a few things."

Kate had heard those excuses before. "That's great, Leo," she said a bit sadly. "I'm proud of you." She checked her watch. It was almost eight. Where were the rest of the guys? "Leo, did you see any of the others?"

"I seen Antoine's and Joey's cars in the parking lot," said Willy Shoes.

Kate frowned. That meant Antoine and Joey Buttons had gotten there before Willy had. "Then where are they?"

"Maybe they got lost," Sonny said.

"Yeah," said Leo with a chuckle. "It's a long time since they been in school."

"Dad, do you have their numbers?" Kate asked.

Sonny opened his cell phone and tried Antoine and Joey. "That's weird. All I'm getting's messages. There a problem using cell phones in school?"

"No," said Kate. "We text all the time."

"Then they must be here somewhere," Kate's father said. "Maybe you should go look for them."

Kate went out into the corridor. The halls were empty, the lights turned low. Having no idea where the other men could be, she started to walk quickly down one hall and then the next. As she turned down yet another hallway, she saw lights at the far end coming from the lobby outside the auditorium. Someone had taped a handwritten sign on the closed auditorium doors.

QUIET
AUDITIONS FOR GUYS AND DOLLS
TURN OFF CELL PHONES BEFORE ENTERING

Kate turned away, but then looked at the sign again. *Turn off cell phones* . . . No, that *couldn't* be why the guys hadn't answered her father's call, could it? The sign was only for those who wanted to audition for the play. Kate stood outside the doors, uncertain of what to do. A middle-aged woman entered the lobby from outside and pushed open the auditorium doors. Kate looked past her and into the auditorium. Roughly two dozen people were sitting near the front of the stage. And on the stage itself, along with Mr. Brenner, were Joey Buttons, Antoine, and another organization guy named Sharktooth Ray.

Kate couldn't believe what she was seeing. Or maybe she could. She hurried down the aisle toward the stage. Meanwhile, Mr. Brenner was saying, "This is great, just great! You men are just what this show needs. But you have to promise that you'll stick with it. It's not going to work if you don't show up for every rehearsal, understand?"

Kate got to the stage. Mr. Brenner saw her. "If you're here to audition, just take a seat."

"That's not why I'm here," Kate said, looking up at the men. "Aren't you guys supposed to be somewhere else right now?"

"What are you talking about?" asked the English teacher.

"I'm sorry, Mr. Brenner, but they're not here to audition," Kate said. "They're here for a really important meeting."

"Whoa!" Randi jumped out of her seat in the first row. She

took Kate by the arm and tugged her off to a corner. "What do you think you're doing?"

"You don't understand," Kate said. "I need those guys."

"No, *you* don't understand," said Randi. "*We* need those guys."

"They're not actors," said Kate.

"They're perfect," insisted Randi.

"They don't belong here," said Kate.

"Listen to me, Kate," Randi said. "These guys have saved the show. Look who showed up to audition. There's no one else to play the parts of the mobsters."

Kate looked at the people waiting in the seats. Most were girls and women. The few guys were slightly built and sort of meek-looking.

"But I need these guys," Kate said.

"Do you remember a promise you made to me on Christmas Eve?" Randi asked.

"Yes, but—" Kate began.

"No buts, Kate," said Randi. "I risked everything to get the information on the Brink's truck route. I could have gone to jail. I could *still* go to jail. And in return you promised. You said you'd do everything in your power. You swore on your pink My Little Pony."

Kate hung her head. This was true.

"And compared to what you asked of me," Randi went on, "what I'm asking of you is hardly anything."

This, too, was true.

"Okay," Kate said. "Let me take them now and I'll make sure they show up for rehearsals."

"Promise?" Randi whispered.

"Promise."

"Swear on your pink My Little Pony?"

"Swear on my pink My Little Pony," Kate repeated.

Randi went to the edge of the stage and whispered in Mr. Brenner's ear. Kate watched the teacher's expression go through a series of changes, from a frown to a scowl to eye-widened astonishment. Finally he nodded.

Randi turned to Kate. "They're all yours."

Kate led the guys out of the auditorium and down the hall. She felt like scolding them for being late for the video conference but knew it would only hurt her cause. Maybe a humorous approach would be better. "So, you want to be in show business, huh?"

"I know this guy from the Tursunov organization across the river," said Sharktooth Ray, who wore a shark's tooth on a gold chain around his neck. "He went to an open casting call for that show *Mob Divorce* and got a small part. Now every time there's a rerun of the show, he not only gets to see himself on TV, but a check comes in the mail."

"What kind of part was it?" Kate asked.

"Part, schmart," said Sharktooth. "All he did was act tough and repeat the lines they told him to say. He said it was the easiest money he ever made. Not only that, but now that he's on TV, he's like Mr. Babe Magnet Deluxe."

"Well, I hope that some big casting agent comes to see *Guys and Dolls* and you all go to Hollywood," Kate said. "But right now we've got to put on a different sort of act."

"So what's dis all about, anyway?" asked Antoine, who'd tucked his long dreadlocks under a red-yellow-and-green-striped wool cap.

"We're going to try to resolve the problem we're having with the Blattarias," Kate explained.

"Here in school?" Joey Buttons said, clearly puzzled.

"You'll see," Kate said, leading them into the studio.

Twenty-five minutes later the videoconference was over, and Kate's worst fears had come true. The conference had deteriorated into a name-calling shouting match that ended with Uncle Benny Hacksaw standing in front of the camera swinging a folding chair and promising to dismember any member of the Blattaria organization who dared set foot in the Blessing organization's territory again.

Afterward, Sonny and Kate each took their own car back home, and met in the kitchen.

"Drink?" Sonny asked.

"Rum and Coke would be great, thanks," Kate said, avoiding the stools next to the littered kitchen counter and instead taking a seat on the black leather sofa in the family room.

"Coming right up," said Sonny. Strangely, he seemed to be in a good mood despite the failure of the video conference. He made her drink and a scotch on the rocks for himself, then sat down beside her.

"Cheers," he said, holding up the glass tumbler.

Kate took a long sip of her rum and Coke, noticing that her father had been less than generous with the rum.

"How can you be in a good mood after that disaster?"

"Gallows humor," Sonny said. "I keep thinking of that idiot Benny swinging that chair in front of the camera and threatening to kill all of them. You gotta admit that it would make any sensible human being think twice."

"So maybe it actually did buy us some more time?" Kate asked hopefully.

"Maybe," Sonny said.

They each took another sip. From upstairs came a loud *clank!* followed by a thud. Both Kate and her father glanced at the ceiling.

"What's with him?" Kate asked.

"I think he's worried he's gonna be short and chubby forever," Sonny said. "He's just trying to toughen himself up."

"You think maybe he feels like he has to get tougher in case Mom doesn't come home?" Kate asked.

"Maybe." Her father took another gulp of whisky. The cheerful mood gradually disappeared. There were too many problems dragging it down.

"What's going to happen now, Dad?"

"I don't know, Kate," her father said. "I truly don't."

Kate finished her drink and went upstairs. She still had work to do for school the next day. Oddly, she felt a tiny bit of hope. Nick hadn't been at the video conference. That meant he was probably still in Vegas doing business. Maybe he was just really busy and distracted. Somehow that made it a little easier to accept that he had not yet called.

He still might.

4

IN THE MORNING, KATE LEFT FOR SCHOOL EARLY.
The driveway was still littered with garbage, but it would have
to wait. She had to meet Teddy in the TV studio. Teddy
would assume they were cleaning up after the FBLA conference. Little would he suspect that a second video conference
had followed.

"Good morning, Blessing," he said cheerfully. Once again he
moved close to kiss her, and once again she offered him her
cheek. He frowned. "Is something wrong?"

"Sorry, Teddy," Kate said. "I'm just distracted by problems at
home."

"Anything I can help with?" Teddy asked.

She smiled. He was such a sweetheart. "Thanks, but I don't
think so." She waved her arm around the studio. "We better clean
up."

They started to fold the chairs and stack them. Teddy had put
jazz on the studio's sound system. He got a broom out of the

closet and began to sweep the floor while Kate dismantled the video camera. As she finished putting the camera back in its case, she noticed that Teddy had paused in his sweeping and was staring at something on the floor. It was a thin copper and gray metal object that came to a rounded point. Kate recognized it immediately: a .22 short cartridge, a favorite of anyone who carried a pistol with a silencer.

"Is that a bullet?" Teddy asked, clearly bewildered.

"Hey, you never know about those FBLA geeks," Kate said with a smile, trying to make a joke. The memory of Benny Hacksaw the night before, swinging that chair wildly—the bullet must have fallen out of his jacket.

"Should we tell someone about it?" Teddy asked.

Kate picked up the bullet and put it in her pocket. "I'll take care of it."

Teddy gave her a strange look. Kate knew she had to get his mind off the bullet. "So what's that music?" she asked.

"Miles Davis," Teddy said.

"Should I know who that is?" Kate asked.

"Not necessarily," Teddy said. "Do you like it?"

Kate wasn't sure. "I have to listen some more."

They'd just finished cleaning up the studio when the bell for first period rang. For the past few minutes Teddy had been quiet and pensive. Kate could tell that there was something on his mind. Now, as they headed for the studio door, she reached for Teddy's arm.

"What is it?" she asked.

Teddy gazed at her with those wonderful blue eyes. "I wanted to ask you something, but then I wasn't sure."

"Do you want to ask me now?" Kate asked.

"My parents have been inquiring about this young woman I've been spending time with. I've been ducking them for weeks, but . . . That's now how my family works. I'm obligated to introduce you."

Obligated? Kate didn't understand. Then again, she didn't really understand the world he lived in, either.

"You're . . . not ashamed of me, are you?" Kate asked.

The notion seemed to catch Teddy by surprise. "Of course not," he said. "If anything, it's them, not you, who I'm embarrassed by. I'm afraid you'll find them somewhat judgmental. But trust me, in the larger scope of things it really doesn't mean anything."

Kate had no desire to be judged by anyone. Nor was the meaning of meeting Teddy's parents lost on her. It meant that right now he was a lot more serious about her than she was about him. But that could change. She liked Teddy. In fact, she was fairly certain that if Nick hadn't come around precisely when he had, she would have been seeing Teddy steadily by now. And given the problems that Nick presented, and the promise she'd made to her father never to see him again, and the lack of a phone call from him in the past seventy-two hours, perhaps it was best to take her mother's advice and move in Teddy's direction regardless.

In gambling they called it hedging your bet.

"So where would you like this introduction to take place?" Kate asked.

Teddy gave her an astonished look. "You mean you'll do it?"
Even as Kate nodded, she felt a nervousness grow inside her.
"They'd like you to join us for brunch this Sunday," Teddy said.
Kate smiled. "I'll be there."

Tuesday and Wednesday passed without a call from Nick. By now
Kate was starting to believe that Friday night in Atlantic City had
been a mistake. She knew she could dwell on her error and feel
miserable, or she could try to think of it as something wonderful,
yet brief. An experience she would never forget and had learned
from. She could look at the glass as either half full or half empty.
Either way it was starting to feel like it was time to move on.

On Thursday Kate left school at lunch time and met her
mother at Il Polino, an Italian restaurant with white curtains and
colorful murals of seaside villages on the walls. Amanda was
already seated when Kate arrived. Kate's mother wore a long-
sleeve white cotton blouse with a camisole underneath, tight
jeans, and high brown leather boots. She looked happier and
more relaxed that Kate had seen her in a long time. She also
looked as if she'd lost weight.

They both ordered Caesar salads.

The waiter returned with a glass of white wine on a silver tray.
"Your chardonnay, madame?" he said, setting the glass on the
white tablecloth.

"Oh, I should have asked if you wanted something," Amanda
said to Kate.

Kate made a rule of not drinking during school days, but life had become so stressful that she was willing to make an exception.

"Could you make it a spritzer?" she asked.

"Of course." The waiter left.

"You're looking well," Kate said. "Is it my imagination, or have you lost weight?"

Amanda nodded. "I've been exercising. So how are you?"

"Better," Kate said. "Thanks for talking to Dad. That was a lifesaver."

"What did you expect me to do? Let you to go homeless?"

Kate found that answer curious. Moving into her mother's new apartment, it seemed, had not been an option.

"One thing you'll never have to worry about is how your father feels about you," Amanda said. "But I hope you did what he said and cut off all contact with Joe's son?"

Didn't have to, Kate thought bitterly. *Nick's done it for me.*

"I know it's not easy," her mother said. "But it's the right thing. I'm proud of you. You're a very mature girl for your age."

So I've been told, Kate thought. Too bad being mature for her age was no fun.

"How are things at school?" Amanda asked.

Kate could see that her mom wanted to exchange pleasantries, but this wasn't the time. "School's the least of my problems, Mom. I know you don't want to hear this, but everything's falling apart. I really wish you'd coming home. The house is a mess. There's going to be a war between Dad's organization and the Blattarias. We *need* you."

Amanda stiffened. Kate wondered if her mother had actually

thought they could get through the whole lunch without discussing anything serious.

"Honey, your dad's been in situations like this before," Amanda finally said.

"No, Mom. Before, when he was in situations like this, he had you," Kate said. "This is different. He's lost without you. He's a wreck. You wouldn't believe it if you saw him. He looks like someone who's lost the will to live."

Amanda sighed and took a sip of chardonnay. "Don't you think you're exaggerating?"

"I wish."

Kate's mother reached across the table for her daughter's hand. "Let's talk about something else."

"You want to talk about something else?" Kate felt all the frustration and anger of the past few weeks boil up inside. "How about this: Where are Dad and Sonny Junior and I going to live after Dad can't pay for the house anymore? How am I going to go to college if there's no money?"

Amanda let go of her daughter's hand and shrank back, obviously unhappy that Kate wasn't willing to play nice. She looked away. The waiter returned with a spritzer and Kate took a long sip.

"I didn't invite you to lunch so that you could be angry with me," her mother said.

"I know, Mom," Kate said. "I want to see you, too. But seriously, don't you think I have the right to be upset?"

"I can deal with upset," Amanda said. "It's the anger that worries me."

TODD STRASSER

"I'm not going to make a scene," Kate assured her. "But I have a right to tell you how I feel. If you can't face the truth, what does that say about what you're doing?"

Her mother didn't answer. She glanced at the next table, where three women had gone silent, obviously listening to them. A long moment passed. Kate and Amanda both sipped their drinks. Kate wondered why their salads hadn't been served.

"It's not really that bad, is it?" Amanda asked in a low voice. "You have enough money, don't you?"

"That's because Dad still has his operations," Kate said. "But once the Blattarias take over his territory, then what? He'll have nothing."

Amanda didn't reply.

"Mom, I don't understand how you can just sit there," Kate said. "It's going to affect you, too. It's not like you have a job or another source of income."

"You're going to be okay," Amanda said. "I promise. Everything will work out."

Kate couldn't comprehend how her mother could feel that way, unless she simply refused to accept the truth. "And what about the house?" she went on. "I mean, you always made sure it was so nice. Now it's a dump. Doesn't that bother you?"

Her mom seemed to wince ever so slightly. "Yes, of course it bothers me. But it's just a house. There are more important things in life."

"I hope you're not saying that because you don't live there anymore," Kate said. "Because I still do. And it's a real drag."

Suddenly Kate realized her mom's eyes were sparkling, not with happiness, but with tears. She could count on one hand the times her mom had cried over the years. Amanda quickly picked up her napkin and dabbed her eyes.

"What is it, Mom?" Kate whispered.

"Nothing." Amanda blinked back the tears.

"Why can't you tell me?"

Her mother shook her head. "Kate, please, can't we talk about something else?"

By now the wine in the spritzer had started to take the jagged edge off Kate's concerns. The salads were finally served and Kate decided there was no use in continuing to upset her mother.

"Did you do something different with your hair?" she asked.

Amanda smiled and self-consciously touched a few blond strands. "I lightened it more than usual. Do you like it?"

Kate nodded. And now she was starting to notice other things. "And your teeth? Is it my imagination or . . . ?"

"I had them whitened," her mom whispered.

Kate wanted to be happy for her mother, but it was difficult, especially when she seemed to be spending so much time taking care of herself and so little time taking care of her family. As if Amanda sensed this was what her daughter was thinking, she said, "Let's not talk about me. Let's talk about you. Are you taking that course to get ready for the SRTs?"

Kate nodded. "They're called the SATs. You took them once yourself, remember?"

Her mother held up a hand as if in protest. "Ancient history. What about your friends?"

"Everyone's okay."

"Did you take my advice?"

"Sorry?"

"I suggested you find someone to take your mind off Nick Blattaria."

Nick still had not called, and Kate had given up on the excuse that he was out of town. If he'd cared at all about her, by now he would have called, and the fact that he hadn't only confirmed her belief that she'd made a mistake. A huge one. The kind of mistake she would never make again. And as far as finding someone to take her mind off him, that would be Teddy, but she needed time.

They continued to eat, and spoke about trips they would take in the spring to visit colleges. And then lunch was over. Kate had to get back to school.

Outside, the sun had come out and the sky was blue and cloudless. In the warmth of the winter sun, mother and daughter hugged.

"Kate," Amanda whispered, "things will be okay. I promise I won't let anything bad happen to you."

Kate understood that her mother meant well, but at the same time, it felt like an empty promise.

That night Kate was in her room studying for the SATs when the door opened and Sonny Jr. came in.

"Out!" Kate ordered.

"But—" Sonny Jr. began to protest.

"No buts," Kate said. "You know the drill."

He backed out of the room, closed the door, and knocked.

Kate counted to five. "Who is it?"

"Napoleon Dynamite."

"What do you want?"

"Can I come in, *please*?"

Her little brother's beseeching sarcasm grated, but Kate said, "Yes."

Sonny Jr. opened the door and came in. He was biting his lips, and his eyebrows dipped with concern. "I think there's something wrong with Dad."

Kate felt a tremor. "Like what?"

"You better go see."

"Where is he?"

"The roof."

Kate was certain she'd heard him wrong. "What?"

"He's sitting on the garage roof."

5

IT WAS IN THE TWENTIES OUTSIDE. KATE STOPPED AT THE front closet to grab her coat and then hurried out into the dark. Just as Sonny Jr. had said, her father was sitting on the garage roof, wearing a black hoodie with the hood pulled tight down on his head, staring up at the starlit sky. He was holding a bottle of Grey Goose.

"Dad?" Kate said from the driveway, her breath a cloud of white.

"They say you can see the stars better in the winter," Sonny said, still staring up. "Something about the cold air being clearer."

"I'll have to remember that," Kate said. "So when did you become an amateur astronomer?"

"They took Pluto away," Sonny said.

"The last I heard, it's still up there somewhere," said Kate.

"They say it's no longer a planet," said Sonny.

"No offense, but that's kind of old news, Dad."

"I grew up with Pluto," Sonny said. "My whole life, there were

nine planets. Then out of nowhere they took one away." Sonny
looked down at her. "They're taking everything away, Kate."

A cell phone started ringing. It took Kate a moment to realize
it was her father's.

"Maybe you should answer it," Kate said.

But Sonny wasn't listening. He was staring up at the sky again.
Kate was worried he might start howling.

Kate's own cell phone began to ring. She checked the number
and didn't recognize it. "Hello?"

"Katie?" A man's voice said. "It's Leo. I'm trying to find your
father."

On the garage roof Sonny lifted the bottle of Grey Goose to his
lips. "I don't think he can come to the phone right now," she said.

"Is he there?" Leo asked. "It's important."

"Can you tell me what it's about?" Kate asked.

"Benny's out of control," Leo said. "The Blattarias have a gambling joint over in Flynndale. Benny says he's tired of waiting for
your father to do something. He's got some guys and they're
gonna hit it after midnight Saturday as retaliation for the
Blattarias hitting Twin Peeks."

"That'll really start a war," Kate said.

"No kidding," said Leo. "By now you must've figured out that's
what Benny wants. He's calling it a preemptive strike, but what
he really wants to do is take over our organization by making it
look like Sonny's afraid to act."

"You wouldn't happen to have the address of the place in
Flynndale, would you?" Kate asked.

"You're not going over there, Katie," Leo said.

"Leo, if you have the address, give it to me," Kate said.

"Your father'll kill me if he finds out," Leo said.

"No one's gonna hurt a girl," Kate said.

"You don't know that," Leo said.

"Trust me on this, Leo," Kate said. "I know what I'm doing."

Leo reluctantly gave her the address.

"Thanks," Kate said. "I'll take care of it."

"Be careful, Katie," Leo said.

Kate closed the phone and looked up at her dad. Sonny was no longer sitting on the roof. He was now squatting on it, like a bird on a roost.

"I have to leave," Kate said.

"Okay," said Sonny.

"I was just wondering if you felt like coming down before I go."

"Not quite yet," said Sonny.

"Dad, sitting on top of the garage drinking vodka is a bad idea."

"I know what I'm doing."

Kate had her doubts. "You're not going to fall, are you?"

Sonny looked down with a frown on his face as if the idea had not occurred to him. "I don't want to break my leg."

"That's the right answer," Kate said.

"Don't worry about me," Sonny said. "I'll be okay."

Oh, sure, Kate thought. *Nothing to worry about. You're just squatting on the roof like a pigeon while it's twenty degrees out, drinking vodka. Perfectly normal.*

She hated leaving her father, but the greater danger to all of them was what Uncle Benny was planning. And that meant getting in her car and driving to the address in Flynndale that Leo had given her.

Flynndale was one of those old towns that emptied out after five o'clock. A few restaurants and stores struggled to compete with the glitz of the new mall on the outside of town, but a lot of the storefronts were vacant. The address Leo had given Kate was a three-story brick building with a shoe store on the first floor and apartments above it. Kate parked and walked through the cold down the dark alley next to the building. Her heart was beating hard and her knees felt unsteady. She was in the middle of Blattaria territory. What if she was wrong about their not hurting a girl? She came to a stairway that appeared to lead to a basement. She took the steps down to a heavily fortified black metal door, and knocked.

A slot in the door opened and a woman's thickly made-up eyes appeared. "Yeah?"

"Is . . . is Nick there?" Kate asked, trying not to stammer.

The woman's eyes narrowed. "Who wants to know?"

"Kate."

"Kate who?"

"Just tell him Kate needs to speak to him and it's important."

The woman stared at her for a moment. "Hold on."

The slot closed. Kate stood at the bottom of the dark stairs and waited. Her teeth chattered. She hoped it was because of the cold and not fear. During her trip to Atlantic City with Nick, he'd told her that he was in charge of all the Blattaria gambling operations. It made sense that if he wasn't in AC or Vegas, he'd be here. But if he wasn't, she could be in big trouble. A minute passed and the slot opened again. This time, Nick's blue eyes peered out. Kate's nervousness suddenly turned to anger.

"Surprise, surprise." She made no effort to hide her bitterness.

"What are you doing here?" Nick asked calmly. Kate had to admit to herself that he was a cool character. Very little ruffled his feathers.

"I know how much you hate to speak on the phone," Kate said pointedly.

"If this is about Atlantic City—" Nick began.

Kate cut him short. "It's about something much more important. A matter of some urgency."

"Like what?" Nick said suspiciously.

"I'd appreciate it if you'd open the door so I don't have to stand out here in the cold," Kate said.

Nick tried to peer past her. "This a trick?"

"I don't deserve that," Kate said. "I've been straight with you, Nick. Which is more than you've been with me."

His left eye flickered ever so slightly. "Give me a second." He slid the slot closed.

Once again Kate found herself standing alone in the dark. But only for a moment, and then the door opened. "Come in," Nick said.

Kate entered a small, smoky gambling parlor with three blackjack tables, a craps table, and a small bar. About a dozen men and women were sitting or standing at the tables, receiving cards from dealers or rolling dice, while a huge man in a brown suit strolled from table to table, watching over the dealers' shoulders. The woman who'd originally greeted Kate stood behind the bar pretending not to see her. She had semi-biggish brown hair and wore more makeup than was necessary, especially since she didn't look older than twenty-five. She wore a tight, red, fuzzy low-cut sweater, tight blue slacks, and red high heels, and sported a set of bright red, clawlike fake nails.

Nick was wearing a black turtleneck and slacks. "Let me take your coat," he said. "Care for a drink?"

Kate started to shake her head, then realized she really wanted one. "Yes, a rum and Coke, please." She gave him the shearling.

"A rum and Coke, Tiff," Nick said to the girl behind the bar, and handed her Kate's coat. "And I'll have a Corona."

Tiff took the coat unhappily. Kate wondered if she was one of those people with a permanent frown.

Nick gestured to a couch, coffee table and a couple of chairs in the corner. "Make yourself comfortable, Kate. I'll be over in a moment."

Kate sat down. The couch was covered with a cheap red slipcover. The table was old and gouged and the chairs looked like they'd been picked up off the street. Kate sat straight up on the couch instead of leaning back.

"I know it's not much in the way of decorations," Nick said, coming toward her with a glass in one hand and a bottle of Corona in the other. "That's the problem when you're running an operation like this. You have to be ready to drop everything and run at a moment's notice." He handed her the rum and Coke and raised his bottle of beer. "Cheers."

Kate didn't toast. Instead, she brought the glass to her lips and took a long sip. Behind the bar Tiff was watching them with what struck Kate as a very proprietary look. It made Kate wonder if she wasn't the only woman in the room whose interest in Nick went beyond business.

Nick settled back into the couch. "I just want you to know that I meant to call."

"Spare me," Kate grumbled. The last thing she wanted to hear were his excuses.

"No, let me finish," Nick said. He sat forward and lowered his voice. "I'm not going to say I didn't have time to call, because I did. It's not about that. It's just that, well, you have to admit that this is a pretty awkward situation considering who our fathers are."

Kate nodded. That much was true.

"So I guess you could say I've been kind of conflicted," he said.

Kate felt her defenses begin to ebb away. Nick was feeling the same sort of turmoil she was feeling. How ironic was it that the very thing that made her feel close to him—their similar backgrounds—was also the thing that would keep them apart?

"You too, huh?" Nick said, as if he saw it in her eyes.

Kate nodded again.

Nick glanced toward the bar. "But this isn't the kind of thing we can fix here, tonight," he said quietly.

Kate was again filled with hope. But that would have to wait. There were more pressing matters to discuss.

"That's not why I'm here, Nick," she said. "I came to make a deal with you."

Nick raised an eyebrow in surprise.

"I'll give you a piece of information that will save you a lot of money and trouble," Kate said. "In return, I need you to agree to something reasonable and easy that will cost you nothing."

"Sounds like my kind of deal," Nick said.

"Then you agree?" Kate asked.

"Whoa, not so fast." Nick raised his hand. "You haven't given me the details yet."

"I know. This will sound strange, but I need you to agree first."

Nick smiled, revealing his white teeth. "Come on, Kate, how am I supposed to agree to a deal when I don't know the terms?"

"You have to trust me when I say it's reasonable," Kate said.

"That's a lot to ask considering who we are and what we represent, don't you think?"

"Yes," said Kate, aware that Tiff was still watching them. Kate wondered if that had anything to do with why she felt so attracted to Nick. Was there something competitive in her nature that made her want a guy when she knew someone else wanted him too? Or was it that she believed him when he said he was also feeling conflicted?

Nick took a long slow pull of Corona, then shook his head. "Look, I'm sorry. I can't agree to that. Even if I did, how do you know I'd keep my word?"

"I think you would, Nick. I think you owe it to me."

He gazed at her with a slightly puzzled expression, then pursed his lips and was quiet for several moments while he thought. "You know what our problem is? Everything is mixed up. It's personal and it's business, and it's hard to keep the two straight. No, I take that back. It's *impossible* to keep the two straight. But when it comes to business, ours isn't exactly known for its high level of moral conduct."

"Are you familiar with the expression 'honor among thieves'?" Kate asked.

"I've heard it."

"We're the future of our organizations, Nick," Kate said. "I have a feeling that one way or another, we're going to be in each other's faces for a long time to come."

Nick raised an eyebrow. "You plan to make a career of this?"

"If I have to." Kate's answer wasn't altogether truthful. She didn't see herself embarking on a career in crime. And she didn't believe that the phrase 'honor among thieves' really meant anything, either.

"So let me ask you a different question," Nick said. "I hear your father's been out of touch lately. People who saw him in the video conference said he didn't look well. Something wrong?"

"He's fine and busy with other projects," Kate said. "He's letting me handle more and more of the local stuff."

"No kidding?" Nick looked interested. "I didn't know he had outside interests."

"It's not like we go around broadcasting what we do," Kate said as she finished her drink.

Tiff walked over from the bar and took the empty glass. "Want another?"

"No, thank you," said Kate.

"So you're Sonny's daughter," Tiff said.

"Thanks, Tiff," Nick said curtly, clearly wanting her to go away.

Tiff shot Nick a nasty look. "Just trying to be friendly."

Across the room a gambler left one of the tables made his way over to the bar.

"Looks like you're needed over there," Nick said.

Tiff rolled her eyes and sauntered away. Nick turned back to Kate. "Sorry, so where were we?"

"I was proposing a deal that would be in your interest to agree to," Kate said.

"The mystery deal," Nick said.

Kate reached for his hand and leaned closer. "Nick, I'm going to tell you for the last time, you'll be glad you agreed."

Nick looked down at his hand in hers and then toward the bar, where Tiff was practically glaring at them. Kate would have bet good money that there was something besides business between the two of them. Very gently, Nick removed his hand from Kate's. "Okay. Fool me once, shame on you. Fool me twice, shame on me."

Kate dropped her voice to a whisper. "Someone's planning to hit this place after midnight Saturday night."

Nick's eyes widened. "And?"

"The rest is up to you," Kate said. "I just want your promise that no matter what happens, no one gets hurt."

Nick rubbed his chin thoughtfully. "What do you suggest I do?"

"You could close up early so no one's around when the place gets hit," Kate said. "Only, if you do that, it'll look like you were tipped off. The smarter play might be to clean out the safe and leave a skeleton crew here to act surprised."

"Why would I do that?" Nick asked.

"To let them think they got away with it," Kate said. "They won't be happy about the money, but they'll just figure it was bad luck—an off night, you know? But you'll know who really fooled who."

Nick smiled. "I like that."

"But you have to promise that no one gets hurt."

"I got you." Nick abruptly checked his watch and started to get up. In a louder voice he said, "I'd like to chat some more, Kate, but I've got things to do."

Kate sensed it was an act. She didn't quite understand who he was acting for, but she followed his lead. Tiff came over with her coat. "Nice to meet you," she said, clearly glad Kate was leaving.

Meanwhile, Nick said something to the big man in the brown suit. The man narrowed his eyes, then nodded. Nick got his black leather coat and told Kate he'd walk her to her car.

"You don't have to," Kate said.

"I've got to go anyway," Nick said. He held the door for her and Kate went out, but not before Tiff managed to shoot her one last scornful look.

They climbed the steps up to the alley and walked out to the street. As they walked under the street lights, Kate kept waiting for Nick to say something, but he remained silent. She found herself yearning for the charming, romantic Nick she'd known in Atlantic City.

They got to her car. She started to unlock the door, then felt Nick's hand on her arm. She turned. His dark eyes were on hers.

"I don't know how this is going to play out," he said.

Kate's heart beat faster. "Are we talking about business or pleasure?"

"Both." He bent down and their lips touched. He pressed hard against her and they kissed more passionately. All the doubts of the past week instantly vanished from Kate's mind. It had never occurred to her that he would feel as conflicted as she did, but now she saw that she'd been self-centered. And that allowed her to forgive him completely. Her passion roared back like an unstoppable river. Was it possible, she wondered, that this was the one true thing in her life right now?

The kiss lasted a long time, and even after they broke to catch their breaths, they held each other close.

"I better go," Kate said at last. She didn't want to, but there was always a chance that Benny would send someone over to scout the place for a few days to get a feeling for the best time and way to "drop in." Kate couldn't risk being seen in Blattaria territory. She unlocked the car door.

"Thanks for the heads-up," Nick said.

"Thanks for understanding," she said, and started to get in.

Nick gently took her arm to stop her. "One last thing. In this business doing things to make sure guys don't get hurt could be interpreted as a sign of weakness."

"So could sleeping with the enemy," she said, and closed the door.

Nick smiled and patted the roof of the car. "Drive safe."

6

ON THE DRIVE HOME KATE COULDN'T STOP THINKING about that kiss and what Nick had said about feeling conflicted. It made perfect sense. Why should she be the only one who felt torn? Of course Nick would be feeling the same way. Not that it solved their basic problem of being on opposite sides in the looming battle between their fathers' organizations, but at least it helped her understand where Nick was coming from. And why he hadn't called.

But was it good news? Or did it only make things worse? Her father had forbidden her to see Nick. That had been awful news at first, but as the days passed and Nick didn't call, it had made her feel a little better about not seeing him. But now that she knew he still cared, that made it worse. Much worse. Now all those what-could-have-beens rushed back, and she felt miserable.

When she got home, Sonny was no longer perched on the roof. Kate asked Sonny Jr. where their father was, but her brother only shrugged and said some of the guys had come by and picked him up. Kate went up to her room, locked the door, turned on loud music, and cried.

The next day at lunch, Kate found herself in the cafeteria, usually the last place she wanted to be. It always seemed like bunching so many kids together at one time brought out the worst in everyone. People who could be perfectly nice in a one-on-one situation became petty, competitive, and nasty when jammed together with three hundred others. And people who were already petty, competitive, and nasty simply became monsters.

Rain drummed against the cafeteria windows, and outside the bare tree branches whipped violently back and forth. Kate and Randi sat at a table near the windows, picking at salads.

"Four degrees colder and this would be a blizzard," Randi said with a yawn, nodding at the rivulets running down the glass. "We'd have early dismissal and I could go home and back to sleep."

"What's been keeping you up?" asked Kate, who, thanks to Nick, had had a pretty sleepless night herself.

"*Guys and Dolls*, what else?" Randi said. "Trying to figure out the set designs and finding volunteers to build them. Derek says that in community theater, being the director basically means doing everything no one else wants to do."

"Shouldn't you be calling him Mr. Brenner?" Kate asked. "At least here in school?"

"I guess," Randi said. "I just forget. I mean, we probably speak ten times a day."

"You must be learning a lot," Kate said. "I just hope it's mostly about community theater."

"Tell me about it," Randi said, a bit distantly.

"Something wrong?" Kate asked.

"Dad's store is going out of business," Randi said with a sigh. "Internet downloads finally got him."

Randi's father had one of the last independent music stores around.

"I thought he was making a comeback with those old vinyl albums," Kate said.

Randi shook her head sadly. "That was just a fad. We had high hopes, but vinyl stopped selling."

"I'm sorry."

"So it looks like the state university for me," Randi said. "And that's only if I can get financial aid."

Outside the wind howled and a tree branch fell with a loud *crack!*

"And you want to know what's almost as bad?" Randi asked. "Taking the bus. It really sucks being a junior without a car. Especially on cold, rainy days. You remember what the bus smells like on days like this?"

Kate did remember, but just barely. It had been a while since she'd taken the bus. But maybe this was the opportunity she'd been hoping for. She leaned forward and spoke in a low voice. "Suppose I told you I know a way that you could get that car. And enough money for any college you want."

Randi stared at her. "Oh, no. No way. Don't go there, sister. If

you think I'm getting involved with another Brink's truck robbery, you're crazy."

Kate put her finger to her lips. "Shhh. Not so loud. What I'm
talking about is nothing like the Brink's thing."

"But it's illegal, right?" Randi whispered.

"Well . . ." Kate hesitated.

"Well, yes or no?" Randi demanded.

Kate didn't answer. She could see that getting Randi involved
in her new idea wasn't going to be easy. But a lot rode on it.
Possibly the future of her father's organization. She had to keep
trying. Meanwhile, Randi gazed past Kate and across the cafeteria. "There's the answer to all our problems."

Kate twisted around and spotted Teddy coming out of the
lunch line with a tray.

"We kidnap him and hold him for ransom," Randi said.

"I thought you wouldn't do anything illegal," Kate said.

"You're right," Randi said. "Besides, things have been hard
enough on him already. Mr. Also-Ran."

"Not necessarily," said Kate. One of the things she'd realized
the night before—once she'd finished crying and gotten hold of
her emotions—was that what had happened between her and
Nick outside the gambling parlor changed nothing. She was still
forbidden to see him and their families were still enemies. Her
feelings toward him may have gone from bitter to bittersweet,
but she was too rational and sensible to get all Romeo-and-Juliet
over it. Like her mother said, her future lay elsewhere.

"I thought that all changed thanks to Mr. Mysterious,"

Randi began. "The guy you won't tell me about."

"Aren't you always talking about keeping your options open?" Kate asked.

Randi grinned. "Wow, you go, girl. So what's the latest with Bill Gates Junior?" She nodded at Teddy, who'd gone to sit with some of the guys from the lacrosse team.

"His parents want to meet me."

"Whoa! Am I missing something here?" Randi asked, amazed. "How many times have you two gone out?"

"Not that many," Kate said. "At first I didn't get it either. But then I thought: How many girlfriends has Teddy Fitzgerald actually had?"

"None, as far as I know. At least, no one from school."

"Exactly," said Kate. "We have to assume that he's had at least *a few* girlfriends. Probably from somewhere else, right?"

"Yeah, so?"

"I think his parents are just being protective," Kate said. "They probably think Teddy isn't that 'experienced,' and they want to make sure I'm the 'right' sort of girl before their son gets too involved."

"In other words, not a gold digger?" Randi said.

"Exactly," Kate said. "And they probably want to make sure that I have manners and know which fork to use and yada-yada-yada. From what Teddy's told me, they have ultrarigid expectations. It was a miracle they let him go to public school instead of boarding school."

"What was wrong with boarding school? I'd go if I could."

"He thinks they're stuffy and elitist," Kate said. "His parents only agreed to let him go to public school because they were hoping it was a phase he'd get over. But they draw the line at college and girlfriends."

"College I can understand," Randi said. "But a girlfriend?"

"Grooming him for the future. Someday he's going to take over the family business, and they expect him to be a civic leader and an upstanding citizen. God forbid he should develop any bad habits—including an interest in the 'wrong' kind of girl, if you know what I mean."

"Right," said Randi. "So where's the big meeting supposed to take place?"

"Their club."

"The Price Club?"

"Very funny," Kate chuckled. "The Eagle Crest Golf Club. Sunday brunch. Women cannot wear slacks and must have the appropriate shoes."

"Are you sure you want to do this?" Randi asked, rolling her eyes toward the ceiling.

Kate wasn't sure of anything, except that the one guy she was truly crazy about was out of reach. So what harm could come from brunch with Teddy's parents? Teddy obviously wanted her to meet them, and he'd been so nice to her. It was hard to say no.

"Uh-oh." Once again Randi's gaze went beyond Kate, but only for an instant. "Don't turn around," she whispered.

A strong mix of perfumes wafted over Kate's shoulder as the BMWs—blond Brandy Burton, blonder Mandy Mannis, and blondest Wendy Williams—arrived. The BMWs were model-thin clotheshorses who seemed to believe that their mission on Earth was to promote the hottest name brands of the moment while eviscerating anyone who dared to think differently. Their parents were all rich and, while the three girls thought calling themselves the BMWs was just ever so cleverly apt, most people agreed that BMW really stood for Bitchy Mean Witches. They stopped beside Randi and Kate's table.

"Look," Brandy Burton said, "it's Randi."

"With her clothes on," added Mandy.

Randi gave them a droll look. "Having fun?"

"Not as much as you've been having," said Brandy. "Who knew you'd be such a star?"

"Sorry to disappoint you, girls," Randi said, "but I won't be on the stage this time. I'm codirecting."

"That's smart," said Brandy. "I'm sure everyone's already seen more than enough of you."

"At least I try to contribute more to society than just prancing around thinking I look hot," Randi shot back.

"That's because you couldn't even if you tried," said Wendy, who, everyone agreed, brought the average IQ of the BMWs way down.

Kate hated the back-and-forth dissing that the BMWs lived for. "Don't you three ever get tired of being nasty and mean? Isn't it time you got lives?"

"And became a future business leader like you?" Mandy asked.

"If only everyone knew the kind of business you're familiar with," added Brandy.

"Yeah," said Wendy with a triumphant grin. "Monkey business."

Brandy and Mandy gave their dim-witted companion looks of disbelief.

"What?" asked Wendy.

Brandy ignored her and turned back to Randi. "I feel sorry for you."

"Bite me," Randi snapped.

"That won't be necessary," Mandy said.

The BMWs flounced away.

Randi turned to Kate. "Did any of that make sense to you?"

Kate shook her head. "Not one bit. Then again, asking those three to make sense is asking a lot."

During the next few days the only good news was that her father stayed off the roof. Not that Kate saw much of him. Nor did she hear from Nick again. Kate felt a cloud of melancholy hanging over her. It seemed like as soon as she and Nick were apart, the sensible sides of their brains took over. The side that said no matter how attracted they might be to each other, there were certain situations that simply didn't make sense. You didn't allow yourself to fall for someone from halfway around the world because long-distance relationships were almost always a mistake. And so was sleeping with the enemy.

On Sunday morning Kate woke feeling apprehensive. She hadn't focused much on the brunch with Teddy's parents, but now that it was only a few hours away, she began to regret that she'd agreed to it. While she felt she owed it to Teddy, she didn't want to give him the impression that she was serious about him. Then again, it was too late to cancel without seriously disappointing him.

While sorting through her clothes she began to think about the questions Teddy's parents were likely to ask, and the answers she could give. By the time she'd put together the preppiest-looking outfit she could find—a knee-length blue skirt and a white oxford shirt under a red and green crewneck sweater—she'd come up with half a dozen good answers. She was upstairs in the bathroom applying a light coat of makeup when she heard the front door open and close. She went to the top of the stairs and saw her father, looking haggard and unshaven, standing in the foyer below. He'd obviously been out all night.

He looked up at her and scowled. "Church?"

"Brunch," said Kate.

"Oh." Her father shrugged his shoulders. He'd always been slightly stooped, but now he seemed almost bent under some invisible burden.

"You okay, Dad?" Kate asked.

"What's okay?" he muttered and headed toward the kitchen.

Kate was about to follow him when she heard the buzz that meant someone was at the driveway gate. She went down the stairs and checked the monitor in the front closet. It was Teddy, right on time. Kate buzzed him through the gates and got her coat.

A moment later she heard the crunch of tires on the gravel driveway. Unlike most guys who sat in their car and honked when they arrived, Teddy got out and rang the doorbell. Feeling apprehensive about meeting his parents, Kate took a few moments more to primp in the front hall mirror, then went to the door.

Teddy was wearing gray slacks, a blue blazer, white shirt, and red-and-white striped tie. "You look very pretty, Blessing."

"You, too, Fitzgerald," said Kate.

"The last time we spoke you said things at home weren't going well," Teddy said a moment later as they drove out the gates. "I hope they've gotten better."

"Just being with you makes things better," Kate replied. It might have sounded trite, but there was some truth to it. As her mother had wisely suggested, it was good to have a distraction from Nick.

Teddy gave her a dubious look, as if he also thought it sounded trite. Kate reached over and squeezed his hand. "I mean it," she said. "I do have some other issues, but I think they'll get solved." And that, too, was true. One way or the other, things with Nick would be sorted out—although, it seemed clear to Kate, not with a happy ending.

Teddy squeezed her hand in response. "I'm glad."

At the entrance to the Eagle Crest Golf Club, they passed a uniformed guard in a booth and drove up a lane lined with large rocks painted white. To Kate's right, the vast golf links were a winter shade of gray-green and lined with bare brown trees. To her left were the tennis courts, also gray-green, without lines or nets. Ahead was a huge, mansionlike club house with blue-and-gold-striped awnings over the windows and a canopy that stretched from the front door to the driveway.

Teddy stopped and a parking attendant in a puffy dark blue jacket opened the car door for Kate.

"Thank you," Kate said as she got out. But when her eyes met those of the attendant, she felt a jolt. "Steve?"

The attendant winked. "Good morning, Ms. Blessing." He closed the door and went around to the driver's side, where he opened the door for Teddy with the same formality. "Good day, Mr. Fitzgerald."

"Hey, Steve," Teddy said.

The guy named Steve got into the Aston Martin and drove it away. What had surprised Kate was that he was their classmate at Riverton High. Parking cars at the club must be his weekend job.

"Isn't he on the lacrosse team with you?" Kate asked.

"That's what drives me crazy about all this," Teddy said in a low voice while he and Kate went up the blue-carpeted steps toward the carved-wood-and-etched-glass front door. "Here's someone I see everyday in school, but when we're at this club he has to call me Mr. Fitzgerald."

"Can't you tell him he doesn't have to?"

"He'd lose his job," Teddy said. "It's club rules. If you think it's weird when he has to call *me* Mr. Fitzgerald, you should be around when he has to call some five-year-old Master Zach."

Teddy held the door open and Kate stepped into the lobby. An enormous crystal chandelier hung above them, and the dark wood-paneled walls were lined with large oil paintings of golfers wearing knit caps, cardigan sweaters, knickers and argyle socks. Tall glass cases were filled with tarnished plaques and trophies. They left their coats in the checkroom and walked past a broad stone fireplace. Nearby several people sat in overstuffed chairs, sipping drinks.

"I don't even like golf," Teddy whispered as they stopped at the entrance to a dining room. Well-dressed couples and families sat at tables covered with white tablecloths and all aglitter with silver and crystal. Heads turned to see who Teddy was bringing to brunch. A gray-haired man in a dark suit approached them carrying blue leather-bound menus.

"Good day, Mr. Fitzgerald," he said, shooting Kate an appraising glance.

"Good day, Peter," said Teddy.

"Your parents are expecting you. This way, please."

As Peter led them through the dining room, Teddy leaned toward Kate and whispered, "Smile, you're on display."

Heads turned and, at some tables, people even leaned together and whispered. Never one to enjoy the spotlight, Kate felt her heart begin to beat rapidly. Had agreeing to this brunch been a mistake?

At a table in the corner, two people sat staring, their smiles stiff and forced. Kate knew instantly that they had to be Mr. and Mrs. Fitzpatrick. They looked like a couple you would find in a magazine ad, sipping wine on the terrace of an expensive resort, or driving past vineyards in a fancy convertible while enjoying the prime of their lives. Even though they were seated, Kate could tell that they were both tall, trim, and athletic. And both dyed their hair. Mr. Fitzpatrick's hair was dark except for the distinguished bits of gray he allowed around his temples. Mrs. Fitzpatrick's hair was a golden blond. Their rigid smiles revealed straight white teeth, no doubt capped.

When she and Teddy reached the table, the Fitzpatricks rose. Greetings were exchanged. "So nice to meet you" and "We're delighted you could come." As soon as they sat down, a waiter appeared and asked what Kate and Teddy wanted to drink. Both of Teddy's parents were sipping Bloody Marys. Kate was briefly tempted to ask for one herself, but instead followed Teddy's lead and ordered a Perrier.

"So," Mrs. Fitzpatrick said, her lips fixed in a rigid smile. "I'd like to say that Teddy's told us all about you, but he's hardly said a thing."

"We hope *you* won't mind telling us a little bit about yourself," added Mr. Fitzpatrick. "One of the few clues Teddy's dropped is that you're in the Future Business Leaders of America with him."

"Yes," said Kate. "And thank you so much for helping us with the video conference."

"Oh, that was nothing," said Mr. Fitzpatrick with a smile. "My friend David Peltz is the CEO of Infocast. All it took was a phone call."

"Are your parents in business?" Mrs. Fitzpatrick asked.

"My father is," said Kate.

"What does he do?" asked Mr. Fitzpatrick.

This was one of the questions Kate had anticipated. "He has his hand in a number of different enterprises."

"Oh, really?" Mrs. Fitzpatrick smiled, obviously pleased.

"Service industry? Manufacturing?" asked Mr. Fitzpatrick.

"Mostly capital management, wealth accumulation, asset preservation, those sorts of things," said Kate, having practiced this answer ahead of time as well.

"So he's a money manager," said Mr. Fitzpatrick.

"Oh, yes, he certainly manages money," Kate agreed.

"Is he with one of the big firms?" asked Mrs. Fitzpatrick.

"No, he's independent," Kate said. "Very low-key and private."

"Good for him," said Mr. Fitzpatrick approvingly.

"And your mother?" asked Mrs. Fitzpatrick.

Kate explained that her mother had always been a stay-at-home mom, taking care of her and her brother, and household affairs.

"I'm surprised we haven't run into your parents socially," Mrs. Fitzpatrick said. "Riverton's a fairly small town. Are either of your parents involved in any social causes?"

Uh-oh. Kate hadn't prepared an answer for that one.

"Are they members of one of the clubs?" added Mr. Fitzpatrick.

"They keep to themselves and a small circle of friends," Kate said.

Teddy's parents exchanged a look. Kate felt as if she'd gotten off to a good start, but now things were turning against her. She glanced nervously at Teddy, who gave her a warm, encouraging smile. Either he didn't sense the change in his parents' attitudes, or, for her sake, he was pretending he didn't.

"Forgive me for saying this, Kate," said Mr. Fitzpatrick, "but most money managers tend to be very active socially. It's part of how they generate business."

"My dad's business is pretty much word of mouth," Kate said, now feeling nervous *and* defensive. Was the whole brunch going to be one long interrogation? For the Firtzgeralds, who obviously prided themselves on being part of "polite society," that sure didn't seem very polite.

"What did you say the name of your father's company was?" Mr. Fitzpatrick asked.

"Mom, Dad," Teddy cut in, just in time. "Kate didn't come here expecting to be scrutinized quite this closely."

His parents politely backed off and turned the conversation to what colleges Kate was interested in. But Kate wasn't surprised when, over poached eggs and bacon, the conversation returned to her family.

"And what are your parents' alma maters?" Mrs. Fitzpatrick asked.

Uh-oh, Kate thought. This was the one question she'd been afraid they'd ask. The one she hadn't been able to think of a good answer to. She glanced at Teddy, who twisted his mouth as if he wanted to help her but was stumped as to how.

"Well, uh, they didn't actually go to college," she said.

Teddy's parents' faces went blank, as if they'd been able to catch themselves before the scowls and frowns appeared, but had no replacement expressions available.

"That . . ." Mr. Fitzpatrick hesitated. "That's interesting."

From that moment forward, the brunch went downhill, with considerably more silence than conversation. Teddy gave Kate as many encouraging smiles as he could, but all she felt from the Fitzpatricks was iciness. Kate berated herself for ever having agreed to meet them.

It was a relief when the meal ended. Mr. Fitzpatrick signed

the bill and they left the dining room, Teddy and Kate first, followed by Teddy's parents.

At the checkroom Teddy was helping Kate on with her coat when she heard an all-too-familiar voice behind her cry, "Oh, Marvin, you say the funniest things!"

Kate spun around. Her mother was coming toward her, her arm linked through the arm of a short, balding, familiar-looking man.

"Mom?" Kate blurted.

Amanda froze. "Kate!" She pulled away from her companion and stared at her daughter with a shocked expression.

A truly awkward moment passed as Kate stared at the short bald man and the Fitzgeralds stared at Amanda. Finally, Amanda said, "Kate, you know Marvin, don't you?"

It was Marvin Goldberg, her mother's dentist. Now that Kate thought about it, her mom had had an awful lot of dental work done in the past year.

Unable to think of anything else to say, Kate automatically introduced the Fitzgeralds to her mother and Marvin.

"Hello, Marv." Mr. Fitzpatrick shook the dentist's hand.

"Hi, Winston," Marvin Goldberg said, and nodded at Teddy's mother. "Tinsley."

"Hello, Marv." Mrs. Fitzgerald gave him a peck on the cheek. It made perfect sense that they knew each other: Marvin was a member of the club.

One of the most awkward silences ever followed. Kate couldn't believe it. Her mom and Marvin, *the dentist*?

"So, uh, nice to see you, Kate, and Teddy, and Winston and Tinsley," Marvin finally said. "Amanda and I better get into the dining room before they run out of mimosas."

"We'll talk later," Amanda said to Kate.

Kate, Teddy, and the Fitzgeralds walked toward the club lobby. "I guess it's been about two years since Betsy passed away," Mr. Fitzgerald said. Kate realized he was referring to Marvin's late wife.

"And your parents?" Mrs. Fitzgerald paused, looking at Kate.

"Uh . . ." Kate had no idea how to answer.

Mrs. Fitzgerald nodded as if she understood perfectly.

Outside, they stood under the awning while Steve and another parking attendant got their cars.

"It was so nice to have met you." Mrs. Fitzgerald said, shaking Kate's hand. Kate forced a smile onto her face, aware that if Mrs. Fitzgerald had approved of her there would have been a kiss on the cheek and a cheery "hope we'll see you again soon."

Meanwhile, Mr. Fitzgerald turned to Teddy. "I'll speak to *you* later."

There was no missing the disapproving tone. Teddy hung his head. A moment later, Steve drove up in a silver Bentley and held the door for Mrs. Fitzgerald. Another parking attendant pulled up behind with the Aston Martin. Teddy's parents got into their car and drove away without a word.

"I'm sorry about that, Blessing," Teddy said, once they were in the car.

"*You're* sorry?" Kate groaned, thinking of her mother and

Marvin. No wonder her father kept saying this time was different. No wonder her mother refused to come back. She couldn't exactly live at home and have a fling with Marvin the dentist. And that, of course, explained the golf magazine in her mother's bathroom.

"Looked like you were as surprised as your mother," Teddy said.

That was an understatement. Kate was still in shock. Her mother and Marvin? It was *beyond* unbelievable!

Neither of them said a word for the rest of the ride home. Kate felt completely humiliated. She'd been insane to ever think that she could fit into Teddy's world. As soon as the car stopped in front of her house, Kate reached for the door handle.

"Don't bolt," Teddy said in a voice filled with compassion and understanding.

It was more than Kate could stand, and she burst into tears.

He held her while she cried and told her he didn't care about her parents, and that he wasn't afraid to stand up to his. When it was easier to go along with their stupid wishes, he usually did, but if he felt strongly about something or someone, he always stood up to them. And in the end he always won, because, as strange as it sounded, they needed him a lot more than he needed them. He was their only son, their one great hope for the future, and the only logical choice to take over the business that had been in the family for four generations.

Kate listened. And somehow it worked. She believed him, and it made her feel better. There were many good things she could say about Teddy, but above all, he liked her for who she was, and no other reason.

"Bottom line is, I don't care who your parents are," he said. "I don't care if they went to college or not. I don't care if your mom is seeing another guy. That's their business, not mine. I don't think of myself as a reflection of my parents. I don't have to believe what they believe. I don't have to act the way they want me to act. And as far as I'm concerned, it's the same for you."

Kate dabbed her eyes dry. Teddy was a knight in preppy clothes, emotionally strong, steady, and reliable—possibly, at that moment, the only reliable person in Kate's life. She'd be a fool not to appreciate how important that was to her.

She took his hand and squeezed it. "Thank you, Teddy."

"You're welcome, Blessing."

He leaned close and kissed her. On the lips. And she kissed him back.

7

AS KATE GOT OUT OF TEDDY'S ASTON MARTIN, SHE
noticed a small green car parked on the other side of the
naked-lady statue in the center of the circular driveway.
The car had a Hertz sticker on the rear bumper. Kate couldn't
imagine what it was doing there.

She let herself into the house. Even with the living room
doors closed, she could hear Uncle Benny Hacksaw's booming
voice. Wearing gray sweats, her uncle was shouting and stomping
around the living room while Sonny sat in a chair listening, a
slightly bored expression on his face.

"It was a setup, pure and simple!" Benny yelled. "We get there
and the place is practically empty. On a Saturday night, for
Christ's sake! There's forty bucks in the safe. Not only that, but
when we get back outside, every frickin' tire is slashed. Every
frickin' one!"

Benny's back was to the glass doors and he didn't see Kate in
the foyer, but her father did. Kate gestured to ask if he wanted

her to come into the living room, and Sonny nodded. Kate opened the door and went in.

Benny glowered at her, then turned back to Sonny. "Someone tipped 'em off, Sonny. Someone in *our* organization."

"What's going on?" Kate asked innocently.

"Nothing," Benny snapped.

"Go ahead and tell her," said Sonny.

Benny laid out the story, which Kate already knew, but she pretended to listen patiently. The night before, Benny had taken some guys over to Flynndale to hit the Blattaria's gambling parlor. The place was empty; forty dollars in the safe. Kate had to admit to herself that the slashed tires were an amusing addition. But while Nick and his guys must have enjoyed it greatly, it created a major headache for Kate, as it clearly implied that the Blattarias knew in advance what Uncle Benny and his boys were planning.

"You understand how this makes us look?" Benny asked.

Kate nodded. Benny pointed a fat, stubby finger at Sonny. "I dunno what's goin' on with you, Sonny, but I do know that someone's gotta do something about the Blattarias. And if it ain't gonna be you, it's gonna be me."

Sonny pressed the tips of his fingers together and gazed at the ceiling. Benny must have expected more of a reaction. The lines between his eyes deepened with fury. "And if I ever find the weasel who ratted us out, I'm gonna saw him into little pieces."

Kate's uncle stormed out of the living room, then banged the front door loudly behind him. Sonny held out his hand, gesturing for Kate to sit. He gazed at her with a half-amused look. A Mona Lisa expression.

"Was it you?" he asked Kate.

Kate nodded. "I was trying to prevent a war."

"Nice try, kid," Sonny said with a weary sigh. "But if it's gonna happen, it's gonna happen, and nothing's gonna stop it."

"I'm not sure I'm that fatalistic," Kate said.

"What's that, an SAT word?" Sonny asked with more of a smile.

"Yes," said Kate.

"So how was brunch?"

The memory made Kate wince uncomfortably, but she forced a smile. Her father knew nothing of Teddy. "It was nice, Dad."

"Good. I'm glad you had fun."

Kate felt bad about lying to him. There was so much he didn't know. Then again, there was so much *she* didn't know, either. Did she really want Teddy? Did she want Teddy to stand up to his parents for her? Did she ever want to see Mr. and Mrs. Fitzgerald again? And what about Nick? If Teddy could stand up to his parents, then why couldn't she and Nick stand up to theirs? But right now there was an even bigger issue on her mind.

"There's something else, Dad. I saw Mom."

Sonny sat up alertly. "Where?"

"At Eagle Crest."

"That's where you had brunch?" Sonny slumped down into the couch and lowered his head. "Your mom invited you?"

"No, I was there with a friend," Kate said. "It was just a coincidence that Mom was there too."

"You believe that, kid?" Her father smirked ruefully. "She left me for a chubby, bald-headed tooth yanker."

"Honestly, Dad?" Kate said. "After all the times you cheated on her? I think she would have left you for the Hunchback of Notre Dame if he'd asked her to."

Sonny frowned.

"It's revenge," Kate explained. "I'm sure she thinks she likes Marvin, and he makes her laugh and treats her nicely, but deep down she's just getting back at you for all the times you hurt her."

Sonny pulled out a toothpick and picked his teeth with it. "When'd you get so smart, kid?"

"A couple of weeks ago," Kate said. "I opened my locker at school and a book fell on my head."

Her father smiled.

"Now I understand why it's so different this time," Kate said.

"I don't want Sonny Junior to know," Sonny said.

"I won't tell him, Dad," Kate said. "But what do you think you'll do?"

Sonny raised his hands, palms up, as if he didn't have the slightest idea.

Kate stepped close to him, bent down and kissed her father on his forehead. "I'll help you get through this. But I better go upstairs now. I've got a ton of homework."

Sonny nodded and didn't budge from the chair. He seemed almost paralyzed—helpless and confused without his wife behind him.

Kate went up to her room and tried to study, but it was hard to focus. The amount of bad news in her life was crushing. The Blattarias threatening her father's territory. Uncle Benny trying to usurp her father's leadership. Her mother with another man. And everyone's parents standing in the way of her seeing the two guys she really liked. Nick was dashing and handsome and sexy. He came from the same world as she did, but it seemed impossible that they could ever get together, given how much their fathers hated each other. Teddy was sweet and nice and funny and smart and a gentleman, but he came from a completely different world, one she could only pretend to be in until someone asked about her parents.

Maybe it wasn't all as awful as it seemed. She had friends, a nice car, and enough money. She liked Teddy, but perhaps she wasn't the one who'd have to change. Maybe Teddy would. He sure didn't seem to care about that world of country clubs and college alma maters and social niceties. Maybe he could leave it behind for her. And perhaps there was hope as far as Nick was concerned, too. True, their fathers hated each other, and the two "organizations" were on the brink of war, but history had shown over and over again that enemies could become friends and allies practically overnight. The Germans and Japanese had been America's enemies in World War Two, and now they were two of this country's closest allies.

Had that been the extent of her problems, things might not have seemed so bad. But the looming "organization" war haunted her. It sounded so old-fashioned and barbaric. People might be hurt or even killed. And since the Blattarias seemed likely to win, her family's business, their home and cars and lifestyle, could be lost. And then what? Would she and her brother and father wind up living in an apartment downtown fighting over who got the bedroom and who had to sleep on the couch? And would there be enough money for her to go to college?

And what about her mother and the dentist? That might have been the thing that threw her the most. It wasn't like she could blame her mom. Not after all the affairs her father had had. But still, to just move out like that completely unnerved Kate. Sure, her mom had a right to be angry at her father. But what about her and Sonny Jr.? Amanda had been the one constant in Kate's life, the one person she thought she could always depend on. Without her the ground under Kate's feet felt as uncertain as thin ice.

Her cell phone rang. As Kate reached to answer it, a montage of faces flitted through her mind—the people she most wanted to hear from. In order, they were her mother, calling to say she'd changed her mind and was coming home, then Nick, saying that he'd arranged a truce between their fathers and things were going to be okay and did she want to go out to dinner that night? And finally Teddy, saying his parents had realized what jerks they were and wanted to ask her to forgive them.

"Hello?" Kate answered.

"Kate?" an emotionally distraught, sobbing voice gasped.

"Who... who's this?"

"It's Randi. Kate, you won't believe what they did. It's all over the Internet. I don't know how they did it. It's horrible. I just want to die. I'll—"

"What are you talking about?" Kate interrupted. "What's on the Internet?"

"The New Year's Eve party," Randi sobbed. "With Stu. They videoed it. I don't know how. It's on the Internet. Everyone's been looking at it. It's awful. I'm going to kill myself. It's the only thing I can do."

"What's on the Internet?" Kate asked.

"A video of me," Randi sobbed. "Someone must have taken it with a camera phone."

"Have you actually seen it?" Kate asked.

"Oh, yeah. Go see for yourself." Randi cried and gave Kate a URL. "I'll run away. I'll go to L.A. and be a porn star. Why not? I'm already a porn star."

With Randi still on the phone, Kate typed in the URL. It took her to an "amateur" sex file-sharing site. And there was Randi, clear as day. The way the camera was angled, you couldn't see who the boy was, but you could definitely see what Randi was doing. The only word for it was pornographic. Maybe Kate couldn't see the boy's face, but she recognized the sea-foam green board shorts with purple trim.

Kate felt her insides twist. She had to assume Stu had known what was happening. He and Tanner and their friends had probably planned it. What an awful, demeaning, brutal thing to do to Randi. Gritting her teeth, Kate wished she could call on Uncle Benny Hacksaw to execute the appropriate revenge.

"Kate?" Randi's quavering voice brought her out of her revenge fantasy.

"You have to make them take this off the Internet," Kate said. "You can sue them."

"Me? Sue?" Randi sobbed. "I don't know where to find a lawyer and I don't have any money. Besides, it doesn't matter. By now they've all downloaded it onto their hard drives. They can send it to everyone they know. It's out there in cyberspace, Kate. Anyone with a computer can see it."

"You have to tell your parents," Kate said.

"Oh, God, no. Are you crazy? I can't," Randi wailed.

"They're probably going to find out anyway," Kate said.

"Oh, please don't say that. Please! Uh-oh, hold on."

Over the phone Kate heard a flurry of keystrokes, and then Randi groaned.

"What is it?" Kate asked.

"Some idiot I don't even know just IM'd me that he's submitting the clip for the home-movie category of the AVN awards," Randi moaned.

"What's that?" Kate asked.

"It's like the Oscars for the porn industry. This is the end, Kate. It's really the end."

Kate's thoughts raced as she scrambled for a way to buoy her friend's spirits. Usually, even with a cloud this huge, there had to be a silver lining. But if there was, Kate was having a hard time seeing it.

Meanwhile, Randi's sobs slowly diminished. "Maybe it's not that bad," she said.

"Huh?" Kate wasn't sure she'd heard her friend correctly.

"Maybe it's not the end," Randi said.

"Okay," Kate said uncertainly, waiting to hear her friend's explanation.

"Look at Paris Hilton," Randi said. "No one had ever heard of her until that tape came out. Now she's famous. And look at Pamela Anderson. Her career was on the skids until that video with Tommy Lee came out. This could be my ticket into show business."

Kate had her doubts, but she wasn't about to argue. If thinking that way made her friend feel better, who was she to disagree?

"Why not?" Kate said. "You've got lemons? Make lemonade. I wouldn't be surprised if by this time next week there aren't two or three other girls we know with videos online. Why should you be the only one who gets famous?"

"But no matter what they do, I'll always be the first," Randi said with a sniff and a chuckle.

"That's right," Kate said. "No one can take that away from you."

"Darn straight," Randi said. "Know what, Kate? You are the best. I don't know what I'd do without you. You watch while I turn this whole thing around. By the time I'm finished, every girl in school will be fighting to get their own video seen. The spin I put on this is gonna make people dizzy."

"Absolutely," Kate said.

Randi hung up. Kate closed her cell and leaned back in her chair. She had to admire Randi. She'd never known anyone who had her friend's ability to bounce back from even the worst possible situations. Kate sighed and felt her body tremble with fatigue. She was exhausted, but maybe she could learn something from Randi. So much of life was a matter of outlook. Why couldn't she see the positive side of her own situation? But try as she might, Kate just couldn't see it. Maybe she was just too tired, but she felt like one of those circus performers trying to keep a dozen plates spinning on top of wobbly poles. Minute to minute there was no way of knowing when they all might crash.

Part 2
Summer

8

"**Y**OU WANT TO BLOW THIS JOINT?" NED YELLED OVER the loud music.

Blow this joint? Kate thought. Had she not known better, she would have thought he was suggesting they smoke some weed, but with his neatly combed hair and permanent-press khaki slacks, Ned was way too straight-looking for that. So it actually appeared that he was asking if she wanted to leave the noisy dance club where Kate and Randi had come to celebrate the end of junior year and dance until stupid o'clock. The club was over in Bronson Park, a town Kate rarely visited—especially since it was in the heart of Blattaria territory—but ever since Randi had gained fame from the X-rated home video of her and Stu, she sometimes preferred to get out of the spotlight and be anonymous.

Kate glanced over at Randi, who was dancing with Ned's friend Bill. If Ned was the straightest guy in the club, then Bill was definitely the runner-up. Kate still wasn't sure how'd they'd wound up with these two. No sooner had she and Randi entered the club than they were corralled by the guys, who refused to let go. At first it just seemed easier to go along with them than try to fend them off, but now Kate was starting to regret that she hadn't put up a fight.

"So what do you say?" Ned asked. Kate decided that "straight" wasn't quite the right word to describe Ned. The more fitting word was "square." Square-jawed, square-shouldered, and square in general. Kate had been dancing with him for about an hour, if you could call Ned's imitation of jumping jacks actual dancing. But at least it gave her a partner and an excuse to move to the music.

"Let me ask Randi," Kate said.

Ned frowned. "Can't you make up your own mind?"

Another problem with Ned was that he didn't know what he sounded like. A lot of girls would have taken a question like that as an insult. Kate did her best not to. She ignored him and moved closer to Randi, who'd clearly gotten the better dance partner of the two. While nearly as square as Ned, Bill at least appeared to have a sense of rhythm. Kate tapped Randi on the shoulder. "Bathroom?"

Randi nodded.

Now Ned will make some crack about how girls always have to go to the bathroom together, Kate thought.

"Can't you gals ever go alone?" Ned asked, as if on cue.

Gals? Kate thought, wondering what in the world she was doing with him.

"Think Bill's kind of cute?" Randi asked as they squeezed

through the writhing, noisy crowd on the dance floor. Randi's gold hoop earrings sparkled in the flashing lights, and her newly streaked hair glistened.

"Definitely less of a dork than Ned," Kate replied, thinking, *Ned the Nerd.*

"But Ned's okay, isn't he?" Randi asked hopefully.

"I won't insist on losing him yet," Kate said. "But I'm getting close. He just said he wants to blow this joint."

"Blow a joint?" Randi scowled.

"No, blow *this* joint," Kate said. "I think it's back-in-the-day for leave, or depart."

"And go where?" Randi asked.

"He didn't say, but if I had to guess, it would be someplace dark, quiet, and private," Kate said.

Randi bit her lip and her eyes widened. "Want to?"

Kate didn't answer. It was moments like this that made her wonder if the word "no" was actually part of her friend's vocabulary. By now they were on the line for the bathroom. "I need to think about it."

"What's to think about?" Randi asked. "We know what they want."

Kate stared at her friend. "Sometimes you scare me."

"What do I have to lose?" Randi asked. "By now the whole world's seen my video. So why not have sex if that's what I enjoy?"

Kate had to admit that there was a strange logic to what her friend was saying. Once everyone's seen the video, why pretend?

"I guess you're just more enlightened than me," Kate said.

"And I mean that seriously. I'm not joking."

"Oh, come on," Randi said. "Loosen up for once. We're celebrating the end of junior year, remember? What could be better than dancing all night and then finishing off with a happy ending?"

One thing that could be way better would be doing it with a different guy, Kate thought. Nick Blattaria, for instance. Only it had been a long time since she'd heard from him. And almost six months since that wonderful night together in Atlantic City.

"If you can't be with the one you love, why not love the one you're with?" Randi said.

Caught by surprise, Kate stared at her friend, who had an uncanny ability to read her mind.

"Gotcha," Randi said with a grin.

Not quite, Kate thought. While Randi had been right that Kate was pining for another guy, she didn't know that it was Nick. In fact, Randi didn't even know Nick existed.

"Come on," Randi urged her. "Teddy's not going anywhere. He'll never even know."

It was Teddy who Randi, and everyone else, assumed Kate was pining for. Throughout the spring she and Teddy had continued to date, despite his parents' disapproval. But while Teddy clearly wanted their relationship to move forward, Kate couldn't quite get past the kissing stage. She wasn't sure why.

By now she and Randi had gotten to the front of the line. A few minutes later, leaving the bathroom, Randi said, "Come on, let's have some fun."

Fun with Ned the Nerd? The more Kate thought about it, the less possible it sounded. There was no way she was going to agree to what Randi had in mind. But she was ready to leave the club. It was late and she was tired. They'd been dancing for hours, and the club was noisy and hot.

They squeezed back through the crowd, found the guys, and said they wanted to leave. Outside on the sidewalk, it was only nominally cooler. It was a late June night and the humidity made it difficult to dry off. Randi pulled the bottom of her expensive lace camisole away from her body to allow some air in. At least it wasn't as noisy or crowded out here. The dark street was lined with parked cars, and here and there a couple talked quietly or kissed in the shadows of a streetlight. Ned and Bill kept exchanging eager looks like a couple of high school guys who thought they were in for their first big score. Kate couldn't wait to lose them.

"You gals from around here?" Bill asked.

"You two definitely aren't," Kate said.

"How can you tell?" asked Ned.

"No one around here says 'gals'," said Kate.

"You're right," said Bill. "We're from, uh—"

"Atlanta," said Ned.

"What brings you up this way?" Kate asked.

"Sales training," said Ned.

"Oh, really? What company?" Kate asked.

"Office supplies," Bill said.

"We can get you a great deal on staplers," Ned said with a grin.

Save me before I pass out from excitement, Kate thought.

"You have to be trained to sell staplers?" Randi asked curiously.

"You wouldn't believe how many different kinds there are," said Bill.

How fascinating, Kate thought. Movement across the street caught her attention. A couple had just come out of a small restaurant. They walked arm-in-arm, talking softly. Kate started to look away, then did a double take. It was Nick . . . with Tiff, the woman from the Blattarias' illegal casino over in Flynndale. They stopped beside Nick's silver Mercedes and kissed. Kate's stomach began to knot. Maybe their fathers being enemies wasn't the reason Nick hadn't called all this time. Maybe it had nothing to do with feeling conflicted. Maybe Tiff was the reason. Kate recalled how jealous Tiff had seemed the night Kate had come to see Nick. What if Nick had been seeing the two of them at the same time? When she thought of that night in Atlantic City, her stomach hurt so much she wanted to cry.

Kate realized she wasn't the only one staring. So were Bill and Ned.

"Someone all three of you know?" Randi asked.

In the same instant Kate, Bill, and Ned looked away, all acting as if they'd been caught with their hands in the cookie jar.

"Come on, guys, let me in on the secret," Randi said.

No one seemed to know what to say. Kate wondered what Ned and Bill had found so interesting. Maybe they were just envious that Nick appeared well on his way to getting what they so badly wanted.

"So what do you say we go back to our apartment?" Ned asked.

Kate felt a deep ache. Part of it was the awful sensation that comes when you realize you've been lied to and used. Part of it was pure anger. If Nick was with Tiff now, then there was a chance he'd been with her last Christmas as well. That would explain why Tiff had seemed so jealous. Part of the anger Kate felt was aimed at herself. She'd marked Nick for a player from the very beginning, but somehow she'd fooled herself into thinking he wouldn't play her.

And that was just plain deluded and stupid.

"Kate?" Randi said. "What do you think?"

From the tone of her friend's voice, Kate could tell Randi was ready to go just about anywhere Bill and Ned chose. But right now the only thing Kate felt like doing was screaming. She balled her hands into fists and dug her nails into her palms.

"Sure, Randi," she said. "I'll go wherever you want."

9

THE NEXT AFTERNOON, KATE DRIFTED IDLY ACROSS HER
pool on a float, sipping a Diet Coke and talking to Randi
on the phone. Usually on Memorial Day weekend Sonny
retracted the pool's roof, and *presto!* the indoor pool became an
outdoor pool for the summer. This year, with her dad so distracted, it had been Kate's job. But then, she used the pool more
than anyone else.

"Were those guys the biggest losers ever?" Randi asked on
the phone.

"Things didn't work out with you and Bill?" Kate said. The
previous night Kate had refused to go to the guys' apartment, but
had agreed to go to an all-night diner. Around three a.m. Randi
and Bill had gone off alone. Ned the Nerd had wanted to keep
partying, but Kate had gone home.

"What a waste," Randi complained. "We parked. I mean, I was
definitely in the mood to celebrate the end of school, if you know
what I mean. And all he wanted to do was talk."

"Are you serious?" said Kate, as she watched a few white puff-ball clouds drift across the blue overhead.

"And not only that, but he asked the dumbest questions," Randi went on. "What did I like to do? Did I use my computer a lot? What sites did I go to? I mean, I felt like he was doing a survey."

That sounded strange. "Did you ask him why he wanted to know those things?" Kate asked.

"Nervousness, if you ask me," Randi said. "They were probably both virgins. Forget them."

"My pleasure," Kate said, wishing it could be as easy to forget seeing Nick with Tiff. But every time she thought of him, her stomach knotted and she wanted to cry. All spring she'd clung to the hope—no matter how unlikely—that someday she and Nick would get together again. But last night had dashed that hope for good.

"Oh, so listen to this," Randi said. "I spoke to Derek this morning."

"Derek?" Kate repeated uncertainly.

"The cute English teacher? My codirector on *Guys and Dolls* last winter," Randi said. "Anyway, the show was such a hit that they've decided to do a one-week reprise in September. Derek wants to know if Antoine, Joey Buttons, and Sharktooth Ray would be interested in performing again."

"I'll ask them," Kate said, although she had little doubt that they'd be interested. Who could have guessed that the guys in the organization would turn out to be such big hams? And that reminded Kate of something she'd been talking to Randi about on and off all spring. "Now that school's over, I really want to do that documentary."

"The nicer side of organized crime?" Randi said. "Hey, I'm all for it."

Kate couldn't blame her friend for being so positive about the idea. After all, in the past few months, organized crime had been very good to Randi. It had taken a lot of persuasion, but Kate had finally gotten her friend to agree to help with her new "venture." They were still in the start-up stage and only a little money was coming in, but once Kate had paid for the high-quality laser printer and small laminating machine, she wisely let most of it go to Randi so she could get a taste of what "the good life" could bring. Hence the new gold hoop earrings, streaked hair, and expensive lace camisole.

"Great," Kate said. "Of course, we'll have to come up with a slightly more subtle title. But at least you've got the idea."

"The thing is, we can't just *say* organized crime has a nice side," Randi said. "We have to find some way to *show* it."

"We will," Kate said. "Every Fourth of July my father's organization puts on a big fireworks display down at Riverton Park."

"Are you for real? I've been going to those fireworks for years," Randi said, surprised. "That's your *father's* deal?"

"He doesn't go around broadcasting it," Kate said. "Let's just say that the people who need to know, like the mayor and the chief of police, are aware of it."

"It's good public relations, right?" Randi said.

TODD STRASSER

"Exactly."

"That's perfect," said Randi. "We can get a camera and go around interviewing people. I bet they'll be as surprised as I was."

"And there's also the Little League team and the annual Christmas dinner," Kate said. "I've talked to Teddy and he said he has a really good video camera. A Sony DSR something-or-other."

"No way!" Randi gasped. "That's, like, a professional-grade camera. How'd he—" She didn't finish the sentence.

"How'd he what?" Kate asked.

"I was going to ask how he got one of those," Randi said. "Then I remembered we were talking about Teddy."

"He's not a spoiled rich kid, you know," Kate said defensively.

"Yeah, right," Randi said. "I'm sure he's very humble about his Aston Martin. Anyway, I'm amped for the documentary. I have to go with my mom to the store in a few minutes, but when I get back I'm going to start writing up questions for the interviews. This'll be a riot."

"Glad you're enthused," Kate said.

They said good-bye and Kate placed the phone by the side of the pool. The truth was, she had a more urgent reason for doing a documentary than just wanting to show the "nicer side" of the mob. All spring the Blattarias had slowly been chipping away at her father's business interests and territory. Instead of the big attack that she'd feared, they'd been gaining ground quietly. Getting stores here and there to start paying protection money to them instead of to the Blessing organization. Moving in on the loan-sharking operations. Things like that.

102

Kate hoped that her new venture might buy them some time, but ultimately the documentary might help her father and his guys move in an entirely new direction. Shows and movies about mobsters and gangsters were as popular as ever and Hollywood was pushing realism. So why couldn't her father's guys get those parts? Who would make a better gangster than a real gangster? Kate had gotten the idea from watching Antoine, Joey Buttons, and Sharktooth Ray in *Guys and Dolls* the previous spring. The guys didn't even have to act. All they had to do was be themselves, and everyone loved them.

If she could get enough people to see the documentary, it just might help get her father and his crew out of organized crime for good, and into organized acting.

The raft drifted across the pool. The warm breeze rustled Kate's dark hair as she floated on the clear blue water. She took a sip of her drink and gazed up at the rear of her house. The glass doors from the family room slid open and two men wearing light blue jumpsuits came out. On the back of each jumpsuit were the words DEE BUG along with the image of a white spider wearing earphones and holding a magnifying glass.

"All finished, Ms. Blessing," said the short, stocky one with red hair. "The place is clean."

"Thanks," said Kate, noticing that the other guy, tall and gawky with a large Adam's apple, was leering at her as if he were enjoying the view of her body in the bikini.

"You want us to let ourselves out?" asked the red-haired one.

"Yes, thanks." Kate turned the raft away so that the tall one had less of a view. She looked up at the clouds again. Each was so perfectly white and puffy. They really did look like cotton balls— except for the thin, misty one that seemed much too close to be a cloud.

Kate blinked. Wait a minute! That was no cloud! It was a puff of smoke floating out of one of the windows on the second floor. Kate groaned to herself and paddled to the side of the pool.

After wrapping a towel around her waist, she went inside and up the stairs. Even before she got to Sonny Jr.'s room she could smell the sweet scent of marijuana. Kate knocked hard on the door.

"Who is it?" her brother asked from inside.

"The FBI," Kate said in the best imitation of a deep male voice that she could manage.

"Crap!" someone in the room whispered. "What're we gonna do?"

"Don't be stupid," Kate heard Sonny Jr. hiss. "It's just my dumb-ass sister."

"Who wants you to open the door, now," Kate said.

"Get lost," said Sonny Jr.

"Open the door or I'll tell Dad about some of the sites you've been looking at on the Internet," Kate threatened.

There was silence, then muttering, then whispers.

"I said, open the door," said Kate.

"Okay, okay, give me a second."

Kate heard a fan start to whir. "Gee," she said loudly. "I wonder why I hear a fan. Did it suddenly get hot in there? Listen, you better open the door right now. I mean it!"

The door opened. While the smoke had mostly cleared, the scent of weed was still strong. Kate didn't dare step in. Ever since her mother moved out, the layer of dirty clothes, CDs, weights, magazines, pizza crusts, and God-knew-what-else on the floor of her brother's room had gotten deeper and deeper. At this point Kate had no idea what she might step on if she went in.

The other kid in the room was Sonny Jr.'s best friend, Tommy Swart, a pimply-faced kid with big ears and the brains of a speed bump. Tommy stared at Kate's bare midsection and grinned. His teeth looked too big for his mouth.

"What are you looking at?" Kate asked.

The smile left Tommy's lips. His face flushed and he looked away. "Uh, nothing."

"Come on, Tommy," Kate said, "haven't you already seen everything there is to see at Hot Babes dot com?"

"Leave him alone," Sonny Jr. said.

Kate turned to her brother. "You and I better talk."

"What about?" he asked, as if he didn't know.

"Just come out here," Kate said.

Sonny Jr. came out and closed the door behind him. Kate led him down the hall and away from the door just in case Tommy was listening.

"Are you completely stupid?" she whispered to her brother. "What did Dad tell you about smoking in the house? It's the excuse the cops need to come in and raid us."

Sonny Jr. rolled his eyes impatiently. Now Kate noticed the hard pack of cigarettes rolled into the sleeve of his T-shirt.

"And you know Dad doesn't want *you* smoking cigarettes, ever," Kate said.

"All the guys in the gang do," Sonny Jr. said.

"Dad doesn't like to call it a gang," Kate lectured. "It's 'the organization.' And just because those guys smoke cigarettes doesn't mean it's right. Dad doesn't smoke, and he doesn't want you doing it either."

"Are you finished?" Sonny Jr. asked.

"No," said Kate. "Your room's disgusting. Mom would have a fit if she saw it."

"But I thought *you* were my mother," Sonny Jr. said sharply. "I mean, you're just as bossy as she ever was."

"Very funny."

"Only it's not funny," Sonny Jr. said. "It's a big pain in the butt. And so are you. Why are you in such a crappy mood anyway? Some guy dump you or something?"

The words hit Kate like a slap. How did he always seem to know when she was having guy trouble? *Was it that obvious?*

Sonny Jr. grinned. "Bull's-eye."

"Congratulations, you're smarter than you look," Kate said. "But my personal life has nothing to do with this. Someone has to keep this family together, okay? Things are bad enough without having to feel like we're living in a garbage dump."

Downstairs, the front door opened and closed.

"Kate?" Sonny's voice rang out through the house.

In the upstairs hall, Sonny Jr.'s eyes went wide with sudden fear. "Oh, crap!" he whispered.

"You better get back in there and air that room out," Kate quickly hissed. "You have any spray deodorant in there?"

"Why?" Sonny Jr. lifted his arm and stuck his nose into his armpit. "Do I smell?"

"No, stupid, spray it in the room," Kate said. "Hurry. I'll try to keep Dad downstairs."

"Kate, you here?" Sonny called again.

"Coming, Dad." Kate headed toward the stairs. Her father was standing in the front hall. He was looking a little better lately. He still needed to regain some weight, but he wasn't as stooped as he had been in the first months after his wife moved out. He'd also started to shave again.

Sonny was holding something to his lips. It was the new Bluetooth headset she'd bought him. "Leo, can you hear me? What? Leo? I can't hear you."

"That's not how it works, Dad," Kate said, coming down the stairs.

Sonny lowered the headset. "I don't get it. If I have it on my ear, then it's not at my mouth. And if it's at my mouth then I can't hear."

"Wear it on your ear, Dad," Kate told him. "I promise, Leo will be able to hear."

Sonny hooked the headset over his ear. "Leo, you still there?" He shook his head. "Lost him."

"You'll get used to it," Kate said encouragingly. "Why don't you try calling him again."

"Doesn't matter," Sonny said. "I'll see him soon enough. Those guys from Dee Bug still here?"

"They just left," Kate said. "What was that all about, anyway? Why are you suddenly having the house swept for wiretaps every week?"

"Just a precaution," Sonny said.

"A precaution against what?"

"Nothing important," her father said.

Kate wasn't satisfied with that answer. But before she could press her father, Sonny said, "So look, maybe you ought to put on some clothes, okay? The boys'll be here in half an hour. We're having a meeting."

"The place is a mess, Dad."

"Hey, it's just the guys," said Sonny.

"Dad, how many times do I have to tell you that you need to set a good example?" Kate asked. "If you want increased productivity from them, you have to make them feel like they're appreciated. If you invite them here, you should make them feel welcome."

"You want me to put out flowers?" Sonny asked with a grin.

"No," said Kate. "Just make the place nice. Put out a bowl of fruit. Maybe some beverages."

"The guys want something to drink, they know how to find the bar."

"That's not the point," Kate said. "You put it out for them so they feel welcome. You want to make them feel like you appreciate them. It's been proven over and over that employees who feel appreciated will work harder than those who don't."

Sonny narrowed one eye. "This is what they teach you in those business classes at school?"

Kate nodded. "And what I've learned in the FBLA."

Sonny held out the headset. "And that's where they told you I should be using this thing?"

"Good communication also increases productivity," said Kate.

"I'll keep that in mind," Sonny said, in a way that led Kate to think he wasn't taking her seriously.

"It's a beautiful day," she said. "Why not have the meeting outside around the pool? I bet the guys would like that."

Sonny shook his head. "Too much chance of someone listening in. Better to meet inside. We just had the house swept for bugs, so we know it's clean. You want to make them feel appreciated? By my guest."

While her father headed for the kitchen, Kate got out the air purifier she'd recently purchased at Wal-Mart. She put out a bowl of fruit and a platter of veggies with a sour cream dip. As an after thought, she put out a small bowl of sugarless gum for Leo Sweets.

A bell rang.

"Someone's at the driveway gate," Sonny called from the kitchen. "Bet it's Willy Shoes. He's always got to be the first one here."

Kate went to the front closet to buzz the gate open. It was only by chance that she happened to glance at the security monitor. The car waiting at the gate wasn't Willy Shoes's. It was Teddy Fitzgerald's dark green Aston Martin.

Kate caught her breath. What was he doing there?

10

THE ASTON MARTIN'S TOP WAS DOWN AND THE BRIGHT sun above highlighted Teddy's wavy blond hair. Kate wasn't sure which worried her more—Teddy seeing her father's associates, or her father's associates seeing him. She and Teddy had been dating steadily for months, and she was fairly certain that by now Teddy had a pretty good understanding of what her father did for a living. But she still did her best to keep his mind off it.

In the meantime, the guys were due to arrive any moment, and she didn't think they'd appreciate having Teddy around while they discussed organization business. What should she do? Pretend she wasn't there? Get on the intercom and tell him to go away? But she didn't want to hurt his feelings. She liked him. If it hadn't been for Nick, she and Teddy might have been a "serious" couple by now.

Kate pressed the button that opened the gate and watched on the monitor as the Aston Martin entered the driveway. Still wearing her bathing suit and wrapped in a towel, she went out to meet him.

Outside, the sun warmed Kate's bare shoulders. She watched as the car rolled up the driveway, the chrome shimmering in the sunlight. Teddy was wearing a coral-colored polo shirt and khaki shorts. He smiled and Kate felt a tug at her heart. He always looked so happy to see her. Why had she wasted so much time and emotional energy on Nick Blattaria when here was a smart, good-looking, sweet (and incredibly rich) guy who was obviously crazy about her?

"I hope I didn't get you out of the pool," he said.

"Oh, no," said Kate. "I was just, uh . . . getting a drink in the kitchen."

"Sorry about showing up without calling first," he said. "I seem to have misplaced my phone."

"No problem," Kate said. "So what's up?"

Teddy hopped out of the car and opened the trunk. He took out a short white sleeveless dress in a clear plastic bag "Ta-da!"

Kate forced a smile onto her lips. She had no idea what was going on.

Teddy saw the confusion in her eyes. "For this afternoon," he said. "Tennis, remember?"

Kate had the vaguest memory of them talking about playing tennis. But she didn't remember anything regarding an actual date. Teddy's smile vanished, replaced by rows of wrinkles across his forehead. "You . . . forgot?" He sounded hurt.

"Teddy, I—" She didn't know what to say. "I'm not going to lie to you. Things have been crazy. I've had so much on my mind. I'm sorry. But I would love to play tennis with you today. Only . . . what's with the dress?"

"It's required," Teddy said.

"It's required to wear a white dress when you play tennis?" Kate was completely confused.

"At the club," Teddy said.

Kate felt a chill. Her last visit to the club had been a disaster. Teddy saw the expression on her face. "You don't have to worry. My parents won't be there."

Kate gave him an uncertain look. "Sorry. It's just . . . you know, a bad memory."

"I understand," Teddy said. "So what do you say? Trust me enough to take a chance?"

He was joking. If there was one thing she was certain of, it was that Teddy Fitzgerald was trustworthy.

"Okay, sure," she said. "Why not?"

A smile reappeared on Teddy's face. "Great. So this is for you. I was afraid you might not have the right outfit."

"That's so sweet." Kate kissed him on the cheek and took the dress. It was plain white and simple. She wouldn't mind wearing it.

The crunch of tires on the driveway caught their attention. An old Cadillac Seville came toward them. It was Willy Shoes' car. Unlike most of the guys, who drove new dark-colored BMWs and Benzes, Willy had stuck with his old Caddy. He pulled up behind the Aston Martin and got out wearing a black polo shirt and black slacks.

Seeing the trunk open and Teddy offering Kate a dress in plastic, Willy made a logical assumption. "You sellin' stuff?" he asked Teddy. "What else you got?"

"Willy," Kate said. "This is my friend Teddy. He isn't selling anything."

"Oh, sorry, I just assumed," Willy said. "My bad, okay?"

"It's no problem, Willy," Kate said. "Why don't you go inside and make yourself comfortable?"

"Sure thing." Willy glanced at the Aston Martin and turned to Teddy. "Nice wheels for a kid your age. This thing hot?"

Teddy nodded. "People say it's a pretty hot car."

Willy scowled. Teddy hadn't understood what he'd meant. But before Willy could explain that by "hot car" he meant "stolen," Kate took his arm and aimed him toward the front door. "I just have to talk to Teddy about a few things and I'll be right in, okay?"

Willy went into the house and Kate returned to Teddy.

"Interesting fellow," Teddy said.

"Quite a character," said Kate. "Always joking around. I mean, let's face it, Teddy, you don't look like the sort of person who goes around selling things out of the trunk of your car. But I really do have to go back inside."

They agreed to meet at the club at four o'clock. Then Teddy got back in the Aston Martin and left. Hurrying back to the house, Kate ran upstairs to change out of her damp bathing suit. By the time she got back downstairs, Leo Sweets and Antoine had arrived. Willy Shoes and Antoine were smoking, so Kate went over to the air purifier and turned it on. Meanwhile, Leo picked a piece of sugarless gum out of the small bowl. "Hey, Katie, you got any *real* candy?"

"Remember, we talked about cutting back on sugar?" she said.

"Yeah." Leo nodded grudgingly, unwrapped the sugarless gum and popped it into his mouth.

By now the rest of the associates had arrived—Uncle Benny Hacksaw, looking surly as usual, Joey Buttons, and Sharktooth Ray. Ever since the community theater production of *Guys and Dolls* the previous spring, Antoine, Joey, and Ray had developed a bad case of what her father called "stars in their eyes." They'd hired show business agents and were taking acting classes. Hardly a week went by that one of them didn't audition for a role in a TV show or movie. Every day they read *Variety* from cover to cover to keep up with the latest show business news.

"You see where DeNiro's gettin' twenty-five mil for his next role?" Joey asked.

"What do you expect, mon?" said Antoine. "Scorsese's directing."

Benny Hacksaw picked an apple from the bowl. "What is this?"

"It's called an apple," said Kate.

"Yeah, I know what it's called," said Benny. "But how about something *good* to eat?"

"Good ain't healthy," Leo grumbled.

"Who wants to be healthy?" asked Benny Hacksaw.

"Benny, if you're healthy you feel better and you get more done," Kate said. "You'll be happier."

"Who said I ain't happy?" Benny grumbled.

"I think it's time to get the meeting under way," Sonny said. "First, my darling daughter has an announcement."

"If anyone wants to go running tomorrow, I've moved the time back to ten in the morning instead of noon," she said. "I know that's early for some of you—"

"That ain't early, that's late," said Benny with a grin. "I usually go to bed by eight in the morning. You're asking me to stay up a whole two hours more."

"Benny, considering the fact that you've never shown up for a single run, I don't see how it would matter to you," Kate said.

"Maybe I don't see the point in practicing running," Benny shot back. "Unlike some people in this organization, I ain't running away from anyone."

It was a jibe at Kate's father, and everyone knew it. Both Sonny and Kate chose to ignore it.

"I'd like to know what we're gonna do about the Blattarias," Benny Hacksaw continued. "Ever since last winter they've been moving in on our territory, and we ain't done nothing to stop them."

"Seems like you've done plenty, Benny," Kate's father replied. "You haven't forgotten about your big score at their gambling parlor in Flynndale, have you?"

The guys smirked and chuckled.

"Very funny, Sonny," Benny muttered. "You and I both know it was a setup. Someone ratted us out to the Blattarias."

"He do have a point," said Antoine. "Seems like they just slowly movin' in and takin' over."

"Sometimes you gotta let the pendulum swing, Antoine," said Sonny. "It's like a football game. For a while one team has the momentum, but sooner or later it swings back to the other team."

"Or it don't," said Joey Buttons. "And it's a total blowout and the Blattarias take over for good."

The mood in the room grew dark. It appeared to Kate that most of the guys agreed more with Joey than with her father.

Then Willy Shoes cleared his throat. "Uh, I hate to say this, but I got bad news for yous guys." He paused to make sure he had everyone's attention. "Things with the Blattarias is about to get a lot worse."

11

"**W**HY?" ASKED SONNY. "WHAT'VE YOU HEARD?"

"Something bad," said Willy.

"Hey, don't leave us in suspense, okay?" said Benny Hacksaw. "Just tell us."

"You know the Fourth of July?" Willy asked.

"No, I never heard of it." Benny smirked. "What's the matter with you? Of course we know the Fourth of July."

"I bet you don't know what the Blattarias got planned," Willy said.

By now everyone in the room was white-knuckled and on the edge of their seats.

"You're right, Willy," Benny growled. "But I know what I got planned for you if you don't tell us right now."

"Okay," said Willy. "The Blattarias are planning . . . a cookout."

The room went silent. The men looked at each other with puzzled expressions.

"A cookout?" Sonny repeated.

Willy Shoes nodded gravely. "That's what I said."

"So . . . what?" said Benny.

Willy looked astonished. "You guys serious? Every Fourth of July we have the fireworks show. That's our holiday! And now the Blattarias are moving in on it."

The other men exchanged more confused glances. Then Sonny said, "Willy, it's only a cookout."

"Yeah, but we let 'em get away with this and what's next?" asked Willy.

"Who knows?" said Leo Sweets with a smile. "Maybe a parade."

All the guys laughed except Willy, who crossed his arms and tucked his chin down against his chest. "Real funny," he muttered.

Sonny let the laughter die and then leaned in close. "It's good we had a laugh, because now I'm gonna tell you why I called you here today. We actually do have a problem on our hands, and it's a big one. As you know, in order to make sure our little escapade with the Brink's company went smoothly last Christmas, I had to pay off our silent partner. Well, someone tipped off the feds and they've started an investigation."

Once again the room went silent.

"The freakin' Blattarias," Benny Hacksaw muttered.

"Don't be so quick with the blame, Benny," Sonny said. "We don't know who the rat was. But from now on we gotta be real careful. No one talks to anyone about anything, got it? And if you gotta talk, it's walk and talk, way out in the open where you can't be overheard. No talking on phones or in buildings or crowds or near cars."

"You think they really got something on us?" Antoine asked nervously.

"No way to know," said Sonny. "But we all know what they try to do in situations like this. They want to make us *think* they got something on us. They try to keep the pressure on and hope one of us will crack and rat out the others so they can get a lighter sentence when the crap hits the fan. And the only way to stop that from happening is for all of us to stick together."

It was nearly four o'clock when the meeting broke up and the guys left. Kate ran upstairs and put on the white tennis dress. She pulled her hair into a ponytail, since on TV that's what most of the female tennis players with long hair did. Teddy had told her to bring a bathing suit and a change of clothes so she packed a small travel bag. Finally, she touched up with waterproof makeup, then left her room. Sonny Jr. was in the hall.

"Why are you dressed like a tampon?" her brother asked.

"Very funny," Kate said. "I'm going to play tennis, okay?"

"Since when do you play tennis?" Sonny Jr. asked.

"I've played in gym," Kate said. As she went past him she added in a low voice, "Don't forget: no more smoking."

Outside, the sun was still high and bright. It was late June and the days were long. Kate jumped in her red Mercedes and drove to the Eagle Crest club. At the entrance she stopped and waited while the guard checked for her name on a list of guests. The gate went up and Kate drove to the clubhouse, where a valet parking attendant took her car.

Teddy came out of the clubhouse wearing a white polo shirt

and shorts, his tennis racket tucked under his arm. He kissed her on the cheek and picked up her travel bag. "This way, please," he said, pretending to be a bellhop, and led her inside. They went down a mahogany staircase to a lower floor where the air had a slightly damp and mildewed scent. Teddy knocked on a wooden door marked LADIES' LOCKER ROOM and a woman in a gray uniform opened the door.

"Hello, Master Fitzgerald," she said. "How may I help you?"

"Martha, this is Ms. Blessing," Teddy said. "She'll be my guest for the afternoon. Would you help her with a locker?"

Teddy told Kate he'd wait while Martha led her into the locker room, which was carpeted and had giant-size lockers with no locks on them. Inside hers was a thick white terry-cloth robe and a pair of white terry-cloth flip-flops. Kate left her travel bag and went back out into the hall where Teddy was waiting.

On the way to the courts, Teddy wanted to stop in the tennis shop for a moment. Inside were racks of white tennis clothes, all featuring the gold-and-blue Eagle Crest logo. Dozens of new tennis rackets lined the walls. Kate assumed Teddy wanted to get a can of tennis balls, so she was surprised when he led her to a display of women's tennis sneakers.

"Let's get you a good pair of tennis shoes," he said.

"What's wrong with these?" Kate asked, gesturing at the light-blue Nike cross-trainers she was wearing.

Teddy whispered in her ear, "They're not white and the soles are the wrong design. The tennis Nazis won't allow them."

The tennis sneakers all seemed overpriced, so Kate picked out one of the least expensive pairs. She wanted to pay for them, but it wasn't possible. Cash was not used at the club. Everything was signed for on chits applied to each member's monthly bill.

"Can I at least pay *you* back for them?" Kate asked.

"No, but you can take me to the movies some night if you'd like," Teddy said.

With her new white tennis shoes on, Kate walked with Teddy to the courts. They weren't like the ones at school, which were concrete and covered with blue paint and white lines. These courts were made of some sort of green hard-packed dirt or clay with a loose surface.

"It's called Har-Tru and it's easier on your legs," Teddy explained. "And someday, if we get really fancy, we can play on those." He pointed at two bright green courts nearby surrounded by a white fence.

"Grass?" Kate guessed.

"Right."

Kate was aware of how often Teddy spoke about a future with the two of them together. She wondered if that would someday be the case. Right now her emotions were still very much tied up with Nick. She knew he was a lost cause and that she had to move on, but that was easier said than done.

They played tennis for an hour. Kate wasn't particularly surprised that Teddy swung the racket and moved around the court like a professional. By the time they'd finished, her face felt red and sweat ran down her neck, shoulders, and arms.

"You're good," Teddy said.

"Liar," Kate said. "Double liar, because you're much better than you said you were."

"Want something to drink?" he asked, wiping the sweat off his face and neck with a towel.

"Sounds great," Kate said.

They sat at a table on a terrace overlooking the tennis courts and had iced tea served by a waiter wearing a long-sleeved white shirt and black slacks. The scene was so idyllic that Kate almost felt like she was in a movie. All those good-looking people dressed in white. The *thock* and *pock* of tennis balls on rackets. The way their every need was so politely catered to by "the staff." It was a different world, not just in terms of money, but in terms of manners and gentility.

"What are your plans for the rest of the summer?" Teddy asked her.

Kate wondered how he'd react if she told him that her top priority was to prevent a war between her father's organization and the Blattarias. Not quite the typical high school summer job. But there *was* the other project she wanted to pursue.

"Remember that documentary I told you about?" she said.

"The one you want to use my video camera for," Teddy said.

Until now, Kate hadn't been sure she wanted more from Teddy than the use of his camera. But if it was as fancy as Randi said it was, she was nervous about breaking it. It would probably be best if she could get him to do the filming for her.

"I want to videotape a fireworks show on the Fourth," she said. "And I could use some help. What do you think?"

"My pleasure," Teddy said.

"Great," said Kate. "I'll tell you the details in the next couple of days. So what are your plans for the summer?"

"Same as every summer," Teddy said. "I'll work at my father's hedge fund. But, uh, that's something I wanted to talk to you about."

"Hedge funds?" Kate said.

"No," said Teddy. "I'm taking the week after the Fourth off and going to my parents' place at the beach, and . . . well, I was wondering if you'd like to come."

Go away with Teddy? It sounded innocent, but Kate wondered if it was his way of gently nudging their relationship to the next level. She didn't know how she felt about that. She needed time to think.

"That's really nice, Teddy," Kate said. "Just curious—which beach would that be?" With Teddy you never knew. It could have been nearby, but it also could have been the south of France or Tahiti.

"Fair Haven, down on Twelve Mile Island," Teddy said. "It's our summer weekend place."

The reason it was their summer weekend place was undoubtedly because they also had a winter weekend place. Twelve Mile Island was just what it sounded like—a long, thin island dotted with beach communities,—from trailer parks and small bungalows all the way up to palatial beachfront estates. Practically everyone she knew went there.

"I'd love to come down," Kate said. "I'm just not sure if I can, or for how long."

Teddy pursed his lips and nodded. Obviously this wasn't the answer he was hoping for.

"It must be beautiful," Kate said.

"Forget beautiful. There's a Momma's down the road from us. The best Italian ices in the world. With old-fashioned custard. You've never tasted anything like it. The raspberry ice with vanilla custard is to die for."

Kate thought back to Big Willy's Hubba Hubba Shack. "You do like junk food, don't you?"

Teddy shook his head. "Correction: I like *fine* junk food. There's a big difference."

They finished their iced teas. "Ready for a swim?" Teddy asked.

Kate was. They walked back to the locker rooms. Kate knew she was catching on to country club life when she automatically put on the robe instead of carrying it over her arm. Strolling through the clubhouse or across the grounds to the swimming pool in just a bathing suit would definitely be frowned on.

As they left the clubhouse, Kate noticed that there were fewer golf carts parked outside. Out on the course, groups of men were teeing off and walking the fairways or riding in carts.

"The after-work crowd," Teddy said.

Ahead of them two men crossed the path and tossed golf bags into a cart. One was short and bald. With a start Kate realized it was Marvin the dentist. She slowed and stared at her feet. Teddy slowed along with her. Marvin and the other man got into the cart and drove toward the first hole. A moment later Kate and Teddy started toward the pool again.

"Sorry, Blessing," Teddy said. "I didn't think there'd be much of a chance of running into him today."

They didn't speak the rest of the way to the pool. Teddy seemed to understand when Kate needed time to think. Seeing Marvin reminded her that it had been a while since she'd last spoken to her mother. After spending most of the winter and spring trying to get her parents to reconcile, Kate had finally accepted that there was nothing she could do. It was up to her parents to either work it out or not.

The large deep-blue pool was lined with white chaise lounges and trees. She and Teddy jumped in and cooled off. By the time they got out, the sun was beginning to dip behind the trees and their shadows were starting to creep across the pool. She and Teddy sat on the lounges, wrapped in their fluffy white bathrobes. High above them, two seagulls circled lazily. After the tennis and swim, Kate felt more relaxed than she'd felt in weeks.

"I know we didn't really talk about dinner," Teddy said after a while, "but I was wondering if you might be available."

"I'd say the chances are extremely good," Kate replied with a smile. "What did you have in mind?"

What Teddy had in mind was a sunset cruise and picnic on his sailboat. The boat was large enough for them both to fit comfortably, but small enough for Teddy to sail alone. With a light breeze filling the sails and the sun turning dark orange as it fell toward the horizon, they skimmed along the bay eating cold shrimp with cocktail sauce and drinking white wine. Kate had a smile from beginning to end. With her cell phone off and her head on Teddy's shoulder, she couldn't remember feeling more at ease.

It was late by the time Kate got home. She felt warm and dreamy and happy. She'd never imagined herself playing tennis at a fancy country club or taking a sunset cruise on a sailboat, but both were surprisingly enjoyable. Or was it Teddy's company that made them enjoyable?

She went up to her room and began to undress. Maybe life with Teddy wasn't so impossible after all. It wasn't the life she was used to, but that could be a good thing. After all, her world was a world of crime, stealth, and secrecy, a life lived in the shadows. Just because it was the only life she'd ever known didn't make it good or right. And while it was her life right now and for the foreseeable future, she'd never really believed that it would be her life forever. There was no special-interest group labeled "organized crime" in the Future Business Leaders of America. She'd always known that one day she would walk away from this and do something legitimate.

She pulled on light cotton pj's and slid into bed. It had been a long day and she was tired. Her head settled into the pillow and she closed her eyes still daydreaming about a life with Teddy Fitzgerald. Something felt strange, and it took a moment for her to realize what it was. Her cell phone hadn't rung in hours. And no wonder. She'd forgotten that she'd turned it off. Kate saw that she had three messages: from Randi, Ned the Nerd, and . . . Nick.

She stared at Nick's phone number, fighting the urge to call back. *Don't,* she told herself. *He's a liar and a player.* Painful memories welled up inside her as she recalled that wonderful night in Atlantic City, and then the horribly painful one just a few days ago when she'd seen him kissing Tiff.

Don't be a fool. She thought of how wonderful and attentive Teddy had been that evening. *You've got someone good now. Don't blow it.*

She erased Ned's and Nick's messages without listening to them.

12

THE NEXT MORNING AT THE HIGH SCHOOL PARKING LOT, Kate leaned against her car and watched Leo Sweets drive in and park his black Mercedes. He got out wearing the same old, stained tan tracksuit she'd been trying to get him to replace for months.

Even though it was ten a.m., the sun was already bright and the day was growing warmer by the second. Leo shielded his eyes from the glare. "What's that big round yellow thing in the sky?"

"It's called the sun, Leo," Kate said.

"It always this hot out?"

Kate had checked the weather that morning. "It's going to be a bit hotter than usual today. That's why it's better if we run now."

Leo looked unhappy. "Maybe I should go back to bed. I ain't used to being up this early."

"Come on, Leo, this will be good for you," Kate said as they started walking toward the high school track.

"I don't see how running around in this heat could be good for anyone."

"Suppose I told you that it would help you live longer?" Kate asked.

"If I wanna live longer, I'll stay in bed."

They reached the track, a quarter-mile oval with a football field and two uprights in it.

"I don't know about this, Katie," Leo said. "I ain't run anywhere except from the cops in years."

"First we'll stretch," Kate said.

"You said I only had to run," Leo complained.

"It's good to stretch first," Kate said as she bent over and touched her toes.

"I don't see nothin' good about it."

"Leo!" Kate said in a way that meant she'd had enough of his complaints.

Kate kept stretching and Leo made a halfhearted attempt to bend over and reach for his toes. His hands barely got past his knees. "You know I could hurt myself doing this."

"Leo . . ."

"Okay, okay. I'm doing the best I can. I'm stretching. It's not like I'm made of Silly Putty."

Kate straightened up. "Ready?"

Leo gave her a woeful look. "You really want me to answer that?"

They began the run slowly. Kate was surprised at how soon Leo started panting, his face red and dripping sweat. After less than fifty yards they'd slowed from a jog to a walk.

"See, I told you this was no good for me," Leo gasped. "I feel like I'm gonna have a heart attack."

"We'll walk the rest of the way and then you can sit," Kate said. "We'll try again tomorrow."

"Forget tomorrow," Leo said. "How about we wait till next year?"

"Leo . . ."

By the time they got back to the bleachers, Leo was dragging his feet. He sat down heavily, his face still red and streaked with sweat. Kate was actually concerned.

"You okay?" she asked while she stretched to stay loose.

"Now that I'm sitting I'm great," Leo said. "Just don't ask me to get up until next week."

"Mind if I run a few more laps?" Kate asked.

"As long as I get to sit and watch, you can run all day."

Kate took off around the track again. She enjoyed running in the heat. It made her feel limber. There were always others at the track, usually a few old folks slowly puttering around, and a few middle-aged guys and women who could go at a pretty good pace for a long time.

"Hey, surprise, surprise," someone said.

Kate turned her head and was indeed surprised. Ned the Nerd was a few yards behind her in a white T-shirt and navy blue shorts.

"You come here a lot?" he asked once he'd caught up.

Kate knew it was no coincidence that he was there. She hadn't listened to his phone message the night before because she had no interest in speaking to or seeing him again. The only way he could have known she jogged here was if he'd been following her. Kate felt incredibly apprehensive. Was he some kind of stalker?

"Only to jog," she answered. "How about you?"

"I try to run a couple of times a week," Ned said. "You don't get much of an aerobic workout in sales training."

"Isn't this pretty far away for you?" Kate asked. "I thought you were staying over in Bronson Park."

"Yeah, I get bored running around the same track all the time," Ned said. "So I try different ones."

Kate didn't believe him. She was certain the only reason he was at this track was because she was.

"So I left a message on your phone last night," Ned said.

"Yes," said Kate. "It's strange, but I don't remember giving you my cell phone number."

"I'm not sure any of us remembers much from the other night," Ned said.

There could have been some truth to that. Kate had had a few drinks. But she was still pretty sure she hadn't given him her number. Basically, she wouldn't have given a guy like Ned the Nerd her number on principle. By now she'd had enough pretending.

"I'm curious, Ned," Kate said. "You tried to call me last night and now you're here running next to me. Are you *sure* this is a coincidence?"

"Well, maybe not," he admitted.

"So you've been following me? Stalking me?"

"No! Nothing like that," Ned protested. "I just remembered

you said you lived around here and liked to jog at the high school track. I figured sooner or later you were bound to show up."

Kate did recall that they'd talked about running. So this explanation at least made sense. But she was still suspicious. "So how many times did you come here before you found me?"

"Twice," Ned said, "and both times I did my jog anyway, so it wasn't like it was a waste or anything."

That sounded truthful. But it didn't change the way she felt. "I admire your determination, Ned. But I'm not sure my boyfriend would, if you know what I mean."

Ned's shoulders sagged a little and she could see disappointment spread over his face. "Oh, uh, yeah, guess I could understand that."

They were approaching the bleachers, where Leo Sweets was sitting checking his watch. Kate knew it was time to go.

"Nice running with you," she said, then veered off. She was glad she'd used the boyfriend line. If Ned was a normal guy, he'd leave her alone from now on. She stopped in front of Leo, but kept her feet moving.

"How do you feel?" she asked.

"Everything hurts," Leo whined.

"It's going to take time to get into shape," she said. "But believe me, you'll be glad you did."

"No comment," Leo muttered. "You need to rest?"

"No, I'll stretch when I get to the car," Kate said. "The walk back will be a good cooldown."

"For you it'll be a cooldown," Leo groaned as he got up. "For me it'll just be another opportunity to get hot."

"I never knew you were such a complainer," Kate teased as they walked back to the parking lot.

"Get me out here again and you'll hear lots more," Leo promised.

They stopped beside his car. "So we'll meet here again tomorrow morning, okay?" Kate said.

Leo looked at her with woeful eyes. "Let's talk about it later. After I get the feeling back in my legs."

Kate laughed and gave him a peck on the cheek. Then she walked back to her car. A sleek bright yellow motorcycle was parked in the spot next to hers, but she hardly noticed it until a voice said, "Pretend you don't see me."

Out of the corner of her eye Kate gave the motorcycle a closer look. Someone was crouched on the other side, as if working on the engine. Whoever it was wore jeans, a black T-shirt, and a bright yellow helmet that matched the bike.

"Keep your back to me and lean against the car like you're stretching." The voice sounded familiar. It took Kate a moment, then she realized it was Nick. She placed her hands against the car and leaned forward, stretching the muscles in her calf.

"Don't tell me you came here just to make sure I stretched," Kate said.

"Look to your left," Nick said, barely above a whisper. "All the way down at the end of the parking lot. The white van."

"So?"

"FBI."

Despite the heat, Kate felt a chill. She grabbed her left ankle and pulled her leg up behind her to stretch the quad. "You sure?" she whispered.

"Look over at the track," Nick whispered, still crouched beside the bike. "See the guy you were jogging with?"

Kate looked. Ned was standing off to the side, talking on a cell phone.

"FBI," Nick said.

The realization hit Kate hard. *Of course!* That explained why Ned was so nerdy, and why he was so interested in her. And why Ned and Bill had only wanted to talk the night they'd gone dancing at the club. And why they'd also stared at Nick when they'd seen him across the street with Tiff. And how Ned had gotten her cell phone number.

Kate took a breath to calm herself. She didn't want Nick to know that she already knew about the feds. "So what's going on?" she asked as nonchalantly as possible.

"Someone paid off the local cops not to dig too deep into that Brink's robbery last Christmas."

Kate recalled Christmas morning and the stacks of cash on the kitchen table. When she'd asked why there two stacks, her father had explained that one was for their "silent" partner. Kate could also recall wondering why the police investigation of the Brink's robbery had not been more thorough. Now she knew why her father was so crazed lately about having the house swept for bugs.

"The feds just love those police corruption cases," Nick added.

Kate stayed silent, recalling Benny Hacksaw's suggestion that it was the Blattarias who'd snitched. And why not? They had every reason to rat out her father's organization. First, because they'd felt from the beginning that the Brinks holdup was theirs. And second, what easier way to take down her father than to have the FBI do it for them? Then the Blattarias could take over the Blessing territory without firing a shot.

"Why tell me, Nick?" Kate asked.

"Why do you think?"

"What? Because you like me?" Kate said. "Sorry, but I'm not interested in players."

"What makes you think I'm a player?" Nick asked.

"Two nights ago across the street from Club Che in Bronson Park makes me think it."

Nick was quiet for a moment. "I can explain that."

"I bet you can," Kate said bitterly.

"I'm trying to get out of that situation," Nick said.

"Looked more like a situation you were trying to get *into*, if you ask me," Kate said.

"It's not what it seems," Nick said.

"Isn't she the one who tends bar at your gambling parlor in Flynndale?" Kate said. "I remember that time after New Year's when I came to see you. She didn't look happy to see me. Like, seriously jealous. So now it's almost July. Tell me, Nick, have you been trying to 'get out of that situation' all this time?"

"Can we continue this conversation someplace else?" Nick asked. "What do you say we get together later tonight?"

"Sorry, I'm busy."

"Tomorrow night?"

"Busy."

"So what night won't you be busy?"

"I'll have to check my calendar," Kate said. Then she got into her car and left.

13

KATE THOUGHT ABOUT TELLING HER FATHER ABOUT Ned but decided against it. Sonny knew about the investigation. Telling him that the feds were trying to get information from her would only make him worry.

The annual fireworks display was held in the town park on the shore of the bay. Traditionally, families arrived around dinnertime and had cookouts, then waited for the fireworks at dark. With Teddy acting as her cameraman, Kate wandered among the families cooking on barbecues and hibachis. Randi had said she'd join them, but at the last minute she'd canceled, saying something unexpected had come up.

"Can I interview you for a documentary?" Kate asked a man wearing a white T-shirt and blue shorts, picnicking at a table with his wife and their newborn baby.

"What about?" asked the man.

"Private funding for public benefit," Kate said.

The man scowled. "What's that?"

"You mind if we have the camera rolling while I explain?" Kate asked.

The young father glanced uncertainly at Teddy.

"We can't use the footage unless you sign a release," Kate assured him.

The man glanced quizzically at his wife, who shook her head. "How do we know this isn't one of those Borat things?" she asked.

"I swear it isn't," Kate said.

"Well, okay," said the man.

Kate gave him a release to sign. Teddy switched on the camera and Kate held the microphone up. "How many years have you been coming to this annual fireworks display?"

"Since I was a little kid," said the man.

"Do you know who pays for it?" Kate asked.

"The town?" the man guessed.

"Suppose I told you that the Blessing organization pays for it?" Kate said.

The man frowned, then turned slightly pale. He held his hand up to the camera. "Whoa, turn this off."

Kate nodded at Teddy to turn off the camera. She lowered the microphone. "Is there a problem?"

"I got nothing to say about the Blessings," said the man.

"I'm not asking you to say anything bad about them," Kate said.

The man shook his head. "Look, I got a wife and a new baby."

"What's that got to do with anything?" Kate asked.

"You better get that release back," the wife said, clearly nervous.

Kate handed the man the release. He tore it up and turned his back on them.

"What was that about?" Teddy asked as he and Kate walked away.

"I don't know," Kate said. "Some people have strange ideas."

But the same thing happened with the next three people they tried to interview. As soon as the Blessing name was mentioned, no one wanted to talk. Finally Kate tried a grizzled old guy sitting in a rickety folding chair with a can of beer in one hand and the stub of a cigar in the other.

"How many years have you been coming to this annual fireworks display?" Kate asked him after he signed the release and Teddy started the camera.

"I dunno, since Sal Blessing started doing it, I guess," the man said in a gravelly voice.

He was referring to Kate's grandfather, Sal, who'd started the organization in the 1930s. "So you've always known that the Blessing organization pays for it?" Kate asked.

"Organization?" the man chuckled, baring yellowed teeth. "You mean a bunch a thugs."

Kate glanced nervously at Teddy.

"It's blood money," the old man continued. "All those nice things them Blessing bastards do—it's just PR, plain and simple. A cover-up for all the graft and corruption and theft those guys perpetrate."

Kate was beginning to regret that she'd decided to do this documentary. She thanked the man and turned to Teddy. "I think we've got enough."

"Hey, I can tell you plenty more," said the old man. "Believe me, I know where the bodies are buried."

Kate felt a chill. She'd heard rumors that under her grandfather the Blessing organization had been far more ruthless than it was these days. But the rumors had never been substantiated. And her father had never been brutal. She was sure of that.

Still, she couldn't help asking one more question. "I'm just curious. How do you know all this?"

The old man took a long pull from his beer and grinned. "I used to be a cop in this town, sweetheart. I know plenty."

Kate was ready to leave, so she was caught by surprise when Teddy lowered the camera and asked a question of his own. "If you were a cop and you know where the bodies are buried, why didn't you do something about it?"

The old man smiled wryly. "Guess you don't know how this town works, do you?"

Kate walked away and sat down at an empty picnic table. This was definitely the end of *The Nicer Side of the Mob*. She must've been crazy to think that she could create a documentary like that. Teddy sat down next to her and rested the video camera on the table. "Blessing," he said, "what exactly is the Blessing organization?"

Kate sighed regretfully. She'd never actually explained it to him. Then again, until now he'd never asked. She'd sort of hoped he'd figure it out on his own.

"In the simplest terms, it's a crime family," she said.

"Like the Sopranos?" Teddy said.

"A nonviolent Sopranos," Kate stressed. It was hard for her to imagine any of the guys in her father's organization actually hurting anyone. With the exception of Benny Hacksaw. And maybe Sharktooth Ray. Or Joey Buttons.

"Seriously?" Teddy sounded surprised.

Now it was Kate's turn to be surprised. "You never heard anything at school? I mean, everyone knows."

Teddy shook his head. "Not me."

Had anyone else said that, Kate would not have believed them. But Teddy was so innocent in some ways, so out of touch with what really went on.

"Well, there you have it," Kate said. "While other fathers sang 'Lullaby and goodnight, go to sleep little baby' to their kids, my father sang 'Alibi and lips tight, make sure they read you your Miranda rights.'"

Teddy stared at her uncertainly.

"It's a family joke," Kate assured him.

"But here's what I don't understand," Teddy said. "If it's a crime family and the police know about it, why don't they do something?"

"Teddy, there are crime families all over the state," Kate said. "All over the country, and all over the world. Just because the police know about them doesn't mean they have the evidence necessary to arrest and convict them."

The lines in Teddy's forehead had bunched up.

"You going to turn hypocrite on me?" she asked.

Teddy scowled at her.

"Remember that speech about how you weren't like your parents?" she reminded him. "You said the bottom line was, you didn't care who my parents were. You didn't care if they went to college or not. You didn't think of yourself as a reflection of your parents, and as far as you were concerned, it was the same for me."

"True," Teddy allowed. "Although at the time . . ." He didn't finish the sentence.

Kate finished it for him. "At the time you weren't including crime families?"

"Seriously, Blessing," Teddy said. "Can you blame me for being a bit surprised?"

Kate tensed. "So now that you know, you're saying what?"

Teddy's uncertain expression slowly turned into a smile. "I stand by what I said. I'm not a reflection of my parents and as far as I'm concerned, you're . . . well, you're just great."

Kate relaxed. She was pretty sure he wasn't just saying it to make her feel better. She gazed across the picnic area at the families huddled at the tables and spread out on blankets. And then she saw something that made her feel a lot worse.

14

RANDI HAD JUST ARRIVED WITH BILL. THEY WERE carrying a cooler and two beach chairs and were obviously there for the fireworks show. Kate quickly excused herself from Teddy, and, her heart thumping in her chest, headed across the grass toward her friend. Now that Randi was involved in Kate's new "venture," there was way too much at stake to allow her anywhere near the FBI.

Bill and Randi were just settling into their chairs when Kate arrived.

"Oh, hi, Kate," Randi said cheerfully. "You guys here doing the video?"

Bill's ears immediately perked up. "A video?"

"Uh, sure," Kate said, realizing that Bill was almost certainly not his real name. "It's about people who pretend to be something they're not. So how's the stapler business?"

"Oh, like I said the other day, I'm not really in the stapler business yet," Bill said. "I'm just doing sales training."

"And which company did you say you're going to work for?" Kate asked.

"Uh, Swingline," Bill said.

"Consumer or business-to-business?" Kate asked.

"Consumer," Bill answered. "Why?"

"Domestic or international?"

"Uh, I'm . . . I mean, it hasn't been decided yet."

"Retail or wholesale?" Kate asked.

"I'll let you know when I know," Bill replied in a measured tone, as if he'd begun to realize why Kate was asking him these questions.

"What's going on?" Randi asked, looking back and forth between Kate and Bill.

"Nothing," Kate said. "We're just talking about the Swingline Stapler Company."

"So?"

"Did you know that you can rearrange the letters *F-B-I* to spell FIB?" Kate asked.

Randi gave her a strange look. "What are you talking about?"

"Ask Bill," Kate said. "Although I doubt that's his real name."

Randi turned to Bill, but he was getting up.

"Where are you going?" Randi asked.

"My guess is to tell his boss that his cover's been blown," Kate said.

Bill narrowed his eyes and gave her a hard look.

"Cover?" Randi repeated. "Will someone please tell me what's going on?"

"You want to tell her or should I?" Kate asked.

But Bill was already turning to leave.

"One last thing, Bill?" Kate called behind him.

Bill stopped and turned. "What?"

"Next time, do your homework. There is no Swingline Stapler Company. It's just a brand name."

Bill swiveled around and walked away. Randi stared up at Kate with a puzzled expression. "Spill."

"FBI," Kate said.

Randi blinked as the implications sank in. "Oh, my God!" Her hands went to her mouth. "Omigod, omigod! Did I say anything? What did I say? Omigod!"

Kate waited on pins and needles while Randi replayed in her head as many of her conversations with Bill as she could remember. Randi bit her lip, balled her hands into fists, and closed her eyes, as if preparing herself for the dreadful realization that she'd said something to Bill that would either tie her to the Brink's case or incriminate her regarding her new venture with Kate.

Finally she took a deep breath, let it out slowly, and appeared to relax. She opened her eyes. "I think it's okay," she said.

Kate realized she'd been holding her breath. She let herself breathe again. Randi sank back in the beach chair as if the intense thought had drained her of every ounce of energy. Kate sat down in the chair beside her.

"That was too close," Randi groaned.

"It's okay," Kate assured her.

"This time." Randi shook her head. "But maybe not next time.

I can't do it anymore, Kate. I'm not a criminal. This is so not my world. I don't have the stomach for it. I don't have the nerves for it. I'm just a simple high school girl. I never should have let you talk me into this stuff. What was I thinking?"

"You were thinking you wanted money for college and nice clothes and a car," Kate reminded her.

"It's not worth going to jail for," Randi said.

"You're not going to jail," Kate said.

Randi stared at her with wide eyes. "Excuse me? Wasn't there an FBI agent sitting in that chair a few minutes ago?"

"But they're not looking into *our* venture," Kate said. "They're looking into something else."

"Like what?" Randi asked.

Kate was reluctant to tell her.

"Uh, hello?" Randi said. "And how many times in the past four months have you told me 'We're in this together'?"

Kate sighed. "It has to do with the Brink's robbery."

"And that doesn't have anything to do with me?" Randi asked. "Hello again? Who got you the truck route?"

"I'm the only other person in the world who knows that," Kate said. "And I've already told you that no matter what happens, your secret's safe with me."

Randi closed her eyes and shook her head. "I can't believe I ever let you talk me into this."

Kate opened the cooler. Inside were plastic cups and a container filled with a reddish liquid. She poured out two cups and tried to hand one to Randi.

But Randi shook her head. "Forget it. Public consumption of alcohol. And I'm under age."

"This is your cooler," Kate said. "I assume you were going to drink with Bill."

"He was probably going to arrest me the second the cup touched my lips," Randi said.

Kate chuckled. "The FBI doesn't care about underage drinking. They have way bigger fish to fry."

"That's what worries me."

"Come on." Kate pressed the cup into Randi's hands. "Relax."

Randi reluctantly accepted the drink.

"To close calls," Kate toasted.

They touched cups and drank. The Red Bull and vodka had a kick, and it quickly took the edge off the tension. Kate relaxed in the beach chair Bill had just vacated. She twisted around and looked for Teddy, but he was gone. Probably for a walk. She'd look for him in a moment, but for now she turned and gazed out at the bay. The sun was almost down. It wouldn't be long before it was dark and the fireworks began.

"There's just one thing I want you to know," Randi said, taking another sip. "You know how you swear you'll never rat me out to the cops?"

"Uh-huh," Kate said.

"Well, no offense or anything, but if I ever get caught, the *first thing* I'll do is rat you out," Randi said. "Believe me, girl, I'm not going to jail alone. First I'll make them promise that you and I have to share a cell. Then I'll tell them anything they want to know."

"Thanks for the warning."

"Look, I'm just telling you the way it is. I'm no tough guy. I have no stomach for this. They put me in a cage, I'll sing like a bird."

"It's not going to come to that," Kate said. "Just don't say anything to anybody and you'll be okay."

They sipped their drinks. The clouds were turning pink as the sun began to set.

"Why the FBI, Kate?" Randi asked. "I mean, I may not know much, but I do know they're not supposed to get involved with local crime unless it's a big deal."

"All I can tell you is, they're looking into a situation," Kate said. "The Brink's thing isn't really the focus. It's bigger than that."

"I hope so, because being investigated by the FBI isn't something I want on my high school transcript, you know?"

"You're going to be okay. I promise."

Randi nodded. "So how's the video going?"

"We ran into unexpected problems," Kate said.

"Like?"

"Lack of cooperation among interviewees."

"Why?"

"People don't want to talk," Kate said, being intentionally vague.

"Oh, well." Randi shrugged and raised her nearly empty cup. "If at first you don't succeed, have a Red Bull with vodka."

They finished their drinks.

"So now what?" Randi asked.

"I better go find Teddy," Kate said.

"Mind if I tag along?" Randi asked. "It seems that I've been ditched by the FBI."

It was twilight and the park was crowded with people waiting for the fireworks to begin. Kate and Randi spotted Teddy at a picnic table talking to "the popped-up-collar boys"—Kate's former boyfriend Tanner Westfal and his buddy Stu, the guy who "starred" in the X-rated video of Randi that was all over the Internet a few months before.

"What's he doing with them?" Randi asked.

"Probably talking about lacrosse," Kate said. "They're on the team together. You want to wait here and I'll go get him?"

"Why?" Randi asked.

"I just thought you might not want to talk to Stu," Kate said.

"I can take care of myself," Randi said.

As they got closer to the picnic table, they could hear the guys talking.

"Now that Richards, Karlenko, and Molinari have graduated, it ain't gonna be easy for us next year," Stu was saying.

"It's a good thing we still have you in the goal," Tanner said to Teddy, giving him a friendly pat on the shoulder.

Kate and Randi joined them. When Stu saw Randi, a big grin appeared on his face.

"What are you grinning at?" Randi challenged him.

"You know," Stu said.

"Hmm, let me think." Randi tapped a finger against her lips. "Oh, yes, of course. People grin like that when they're embarrassed.

Now, what could you possibly be embarrassed about? Size, or lack thereof? Well, that's perfectly understandable in your case."

Now it was Tanner's turn to grin. Teddy politely covered his lips with his hand to hide his smile. Even in the dim light Kate could see that Stu's face had turned bright red.

"Have you considered surgical enhancement?" Randi went on. "It's amazing what they can do these days. Even in a case like yours."

By now Tanner was smirking. Teddy turned away so that they couldn't see his face. Stu's mouth fell open as if he wanted to reply, but the words weren't coming.

"You're not trying to say something, are you?" Randi asked him. "You know, chances are that if you're small in one place, you're probably small in another. That could include your brain."

"You know, you . . . you . . . ," Stu stammered.

"Easy now, Stu," Randi said, "try to stay calm. Don't strain yourself."

"You can say whatever you want," Stu said. "But it's *always* gonna be you on that video, Randi. For *everyone* to see."

Randi's eyes narrowed and Kate knew that as feeble as Stu's reply had been, it still stung.

Now Kate became aware of another presence approaching. The BMWs were making their way through the crowd. All three were dressed in pastel capris and tight spaghetti-strap tops.

"Well, well," Brandy Burton grinned meanly. "It's Randi-Does-Riverton. Where have you been hiding?"

Kate felt terrible for her friend.

"I haven't been hiding anywhere," Randi shot back. "You know, just because I got caught on tape and you didn't doesn't make you a better person. Everyone knows you'll go with anything in pants."

"Look who's talking," said Mandy Mannis. "Although I do have to say that you're looking awfully good these days. The clothes and hair and jewelry really look fabulous. And at a time when your father's business is in the toilet. I mean, how do you explain it? You haven't gone pro, have you?"

With a scowl on her face, Wendy Williams turned to her friends. "You mean, professional? Like in sports?"

Stu sniggered. "The only sport Randi knows is one you have to perform on your back."

Wendy was clearly puzzled. "The backstroke?"

Her friends rolled their eyes. With the brains of a tree stump, Wendy could have been the butt of every blonde joke ever told.

"Okay, I hope everyone's had a good time," Teddy said, starting to move toward Kate and Randi. He waved to the others. "Have a good summer."

"We will," Brandy said. "It's supposed to be in the nineties next week and we're all going to Wendy's parents' beach house in Oceandale."

"Gee, Wendy," Randi began, "I always wondered—" But she didn't finish the sentence.

"Wondered what?" Wendy asked.

"Forget it," Randi said. "Have fun at the beach. Try not to get sand in those sensitive places."

Teddy, Kate, and Randi strolled away. When they were out of

earshot, Kate said to Randi, "You were going to say that you always wondered why they put up with Wendy, right?"

Randi nodded.

"You mean, because they like going to her beach house?" Teddy guessed.

"Can you think of any other reason?" Kate asked, then turned to Randi. "So why didn't you say it?"

"Too mean," Randi said. "What's the point? It's not Wendy's fault that she's not a rocket scientist."

They stayed for the fireworks show, then walked with the crowd through the dark and drifting clouds of burnt gunpowder toward the parking lot. Randi wanted to go home. Kate didn't mind. She wanted to be alone with Teddy.

They'd just dropped Randi at her house when Kate's cell phone rang. The number looked oddly familiar. "Hello?"

"Kate Blessing?" a deep male voice said.

"Yes?"

"This is Sergeant Lawson down at the Riverton PD," the man said.

Now Kate knew why the number looked familiar. It was printed in big black letters on the side of every patrol car in Riverton.

15

KATE FELT HERSELF GO RIGID. HAD THE BLATTARIAS put a hit on her father? Had something bad happened to her mother? Her grip on the cell phone tightened.

"I'm sorry to bother you," Sergeant Lawson said, "but we've got your brother down here. We've been trying to find your parents and we can't locate either of them."

"What's this about?" Kate asked.

"I'd rather not say over the phone," the sergeant said. "The problem is, if you can't get down here pretty soon, we'll have to hold him overnight."

"Did something happen?" Kate asked. "Why is he there?"

"We'll tell you when you get down here, okay?" Lawson said.

They drove toward town. Kate told herself to relax. There was no point in getting freaked until she knew what the story was. At least no one had been hurt. With the top down she felt the warm July air on her face. Most of the organized fireworks shows were over by now, but from the dark came the loud booms of privately owned M-80s and cherry bombs, the *rat-tit-tat-tat* of firecrackers, and the sparkling *whoosh* of bottle rockets against the dark sky.

The police station was a small white building with a covered portico outside. "Want me to wait out here?" Teddy asked.

Kate knew he was trying to be polite, but she trusted him, and it could be helpful if he were with her. They went in together. Kate told the dispatcher who she was, then waited on a wooden bench with Teddy, who held her hand reassuringly. A short time later a door opened and Sonny Jr. came out with a tall, dark-haired police officer wearing a dark blue uniform. He had a moustache and a broad round belly.

"Ms. Blessing?" the officer extended his hand. "I'm Sergeant Lawson."

Kate shook his hand and glanced at Sonny Jr., who averted his eyes.

"I'm afraid your brother has gotten himself into a bit of trouble," Lawson said. "It's something I'd rather speak to your parents about, but I'm going off duty in a few minutes and I'd hate to have to put him in lockup until the morning."

"Is that where he's been?" Kate asked, alarmed that they'd put Sonny Jr. in an actual jail cell. "I mean, since he's been here?"

"Oh, no," said the police sergeant. "I've had him at my desk up till now. He's been reading through our lists of wanted suspects."

Sonny Jr. kept his head bent and his eyes glued to the floor.

"What happened?" Kate asked.

"Your brother and his friends got into a couple of six-packs and then went around town shooting at parked cars and houses with a paintball gun. They made quite a mess."

Kate stared at her brother in disbelief. Sonny Jr. scuffed his shoe against the floor. The Fourth of July was traditionally the night when the Blessings did something nice for the town. Kate hated to think how her father would react when he learned that his son had been vandalizing cars and houses.

"Could you and I speak in private?" Lawson asked, pushing open the door he and Sonny Jr. had come through earlier.

The suggestion caught Kate by surprise, but she quickly nodded.

"I'll keep an eye on him," Teddy offered.

Kate followed the sergeant into a large room filled with desks, each with a computer, a phone, and piles of papers. Kate assumed they would go to one of the desks, but Lawson led her through yet another doorway and into a narrow, brightly lit hallway. He stopped and pressed his back against the wall. It was clear to Kate that he wanted to speak in private.

"So, Ms. Blessing," the sergeant began in a low voice.

"Please call me Kate."

"Uh, Kate, so here's the deal. Normally in a situation like this, where there's been underage drinking and vandalism, we are required to press charges. But in this case, since we know the family, I think we'll be willing to let your brother go with a warning. Provided, of course, that we know that you'll take this incident seriously."

"Believe me, sergeant, my father will take this very seriously," Kate assured him.

Lawson paused thoughtfully, then said, "So how's your dad doing?"

Kate knew this was more than a mere polite inquiry. "He's fine, sir. I guess you know he went through a rough patch recently, but that's behind him now. He's very solid."

"Word has it that you've been a great help to him," Lawson said.

"Just trying to be a good daughter, sir," Kate said.

The sergeant paused again. It seemed to Kate as if he were taking tentative, uncertain steps. "So, uh, since you've been working closely with your father, I assume you're aware that things have gotten a bit sticky around here?"

He was referring to the FBI investigation. This was *uber*-serious stuff. "Yes, sir. We've discussed it and we're confident that we can ride it out."

"A lot of people are depending on that," Lawson said.

"My father is a very honorable man," Kate said. "You can count on him to do the right thing."

Lawson nodded, then opened the door. The discussion was over. Back at the dispatcher's desk, the police sergeant had a few final words with Sonny Jr. to make sure he understood that if he ever got caught vandalizing or drinking again there'd be big trouble. Then she, Teddy, and Sonny Jr. left. Outside in the dark, the sky no longer flickered with the occasional rocket, but the pops and booms of fireworks could still be heard. When they got to Teddy's car. Sonny Jr.'s jaw dropped. "No way! An Aston Martin!? Like what James Bond used to drive!"

STOLEN KISSES, SECRETS, AND LIES

"He drove a DB5," said Teddy.

"They had it in *Casino Royale*," Kate's brother said excitedly. "Along with that really new one."

"The DBS," said Teddy. "Is that thing a monster or what?"

"Totally gruesome!" Sonny Jr. agreed with more enthusiasm than Kate had witnessed in who knew how long. "So what's this?"

"A DB9," Teddy said.

"How much horsepower?" Kate's brother asked as they got in.

"Around four-fifty," Teddy said.

"Awesome! Let's leave tracks!"

Kate and Teddy smiled at each other. "Tell you what," Teddy said as they started toward home. "Maybe one of these days we'll go over to the high school and you can drive around the parking lot. What do you say?"

"Serious?" Sonny Jr. gasped from the backseat. "That would be gruesome cool!"

Kate would not have guessed that a car could make her brother so excited. But as they rode through the dark, Sonny Jr. became quiet, and then he asked, "You're not gonna tell Dad, are you?"

Kate would have said that she'd promised Sgt. Lawson, but Teddy caught her eye and shook his head slightly. It only took her a second to catch on.

"Suppose I don't," she said. "Am I ever going to find you smoking anything in our house again?"

"No way," said Sonny Jr.

"Am I ever going to hear about you drinking again?"

"Nope."

"Getting into any kind of trouble with your friends?"

"Nuh-uh."

"Because if I do—" Kate began.

"You'll tell Dad," Sonny Jr. finished the sentence for her.

They returned to silence, but not for long. Teddy looked in the rearview mirror at Sonny Jr. "Do you have anything to do this summer?"

"Like what?"

"Like a job or anything?" Teddy asked.

Sonny Jr. shook his head.

"You lift?" Teddy asked.

"How'd you know?" Sonny Jr. asked, surprised.

"Lucky guess," Teddy said. "How'd you like to lift this summer *and* build your endurance *and* get paid for doing it while enjoying the great out-of-doors?"

"What are you talking about?" Sonny Jr. asked. Kate couldn't figure out what Teddy was talking about either.

"A job," Teddy said.

"There's no job that'll pay me to do that," said Sonny Jr.

"Sure there is," said Teddy.

When they got back to the house, Sonny Jr. went in, but Kate lingered in the car with Teddy. "Thanks for all your help tonight."

"Any time," Teddy replied. "What do you think you'll do about the documentary?"

Kate had hardly had time to think about it. Way too much had happened tonight—the scene with the BMWs, saving Randi from Bill, getting Sonny Jr. at the police station. She felt like her brain was on overload. "Hard to focus on it right now."

Teddy smiled at her. "Some night, huh?"

"I'll say." She let her head tilt against the headrest and smiled back. Suddenly what had seemed like a nightmarish evening was turning dreamy. They were alone in the car. It was quiet. The top was down and the dark air was warm and moist. Now and then the distant boom of a cherry bomb broke the silence.

"What is it with guys and fireworks?" Kate asked languidly.

"There's just something irresistible about blowing stuff up."

"Such a male thing," Kate said.

"Boys will be boys."

Kate gazed softly at him. "How come you never strike me as a boy?"

"Maybe you just haven't seen that side of me," Teddy said.

"I think I would have, by now," Kate said. A sudden urge seized her and she leaned toward him. "And that reminds me. There's another side of you I definitely haven't seen enough of."

They kissed for a long time. As always, Teddy was courteous to a fault. He was a good kisser, but he hesitated to take things further. Kate finally had to take his hand and place it where she was willing to let it go. And even then he seemed reluctant to proceed. It made Kate wonder. He'd never had girlfriends at school, but he was so good-looking and charming that she'd naturally assumed he'd had them in other places—camp, or the daughters of family friends, or whatever. But maybe not. And that made him so different from Nick, whose confidence flowed in situations like this.

Nick had intuition; he knew when to go further and just how far to go. She didn't even have to think when she was with him. She just let him take over.

Even now she could imagine him kissing her, running his hands over her body, his hot breath in her ear. She missed him. She hated to admit it, but she did.

Teddy stopped kissing her. When she opened her eyes, he was giving her an odd look.

"Something wrong?" Kate asked.

"Did you just call me Nick?"

Kate forced a laugh while her brain raced. "I probably meant, in the nick of time, or something."

"Why?"

"Oh, I don't know," Kate said. "I guess it seemed like this whole night was going so wrong, and then there you were holding me and kissing me just in the nick of time."

She forced a smile, but inside she was tensing. *Did he believe her?*

He kissed her lightly on the lips. "You say some funny things."

Phew! Kate went limp with relief.

Later, after Teddy left, she went into the kitchen. Sonny Jr. was sitting on the couch in the family room watching *South Park*.

"Is he your new boyfriend?" he asked.

"Good question," Kate replied.

"He's a cool guy," Sonny Jr. said.

"Because you like his car?" Kate asked.

"No," said her brother. "He's just cool. Trust me, I know."

16

"SON OF A BITCH!"

Kate opened her eyes. Bright morning sunlight peaked in around the blinds in her room. She yawned. Had she really heard her father cursing downstairs? Or had she dreamed it?

"Damn it!"

That was no dream. Sonny was definitely cursing. It wasn't like her father to get that upset. Kate assumed that he must have just learned about Sonny Jr.'s antics the night before, but his reaction still sounded out of proportion. She quickly pulled on her robe and hurried downstairs. Her father was in the kitchen, one hand holding the phone, the other balled so tightly into a fist that the knuckles were white.

"Damn it!" he yelled again, snapping the phone shut.

"Dad, if it's about Sonny Junior," Kate said, "I—"

"They hit the factory," her father muttered. He placed his hands flat on the kitchen counter and leaned against it, as if he needed it to steady himself. "They took everything—the knocked-off goods, the DVD copiers, even the sewing machines."

Kate stopped. The factory was the backbone of her father's operations. It was the place where all the knockoff designer bags and jeans and polo shirts were made, as well as where the pirated CDs and DVDs were produced. The factory was so crucial to the organization's income that its location was a secret. Only a few of the "associates" knew where it was, and they were forbidden to talk about it. Kate had never seen it, and the only reason she knew it existed was because she'd overheard her mother and father discussing it.

Sonny stared at the kitchen counter and said nothing. Kate knew better than to talk.

The phone rang again. "What?" Sonny answered angrily. "Yeah, okay. Right. I'll be there."

He shut the phone, then looked at Kate. "Get dressed. We gotta go to Quik Nail."

Kate hurried back upstairs and threw on a T-shirt and a pair of jeans. A few minutes later she was in the passenger seat of her father's BMW, heading toward town.

"Someone talked," her father muttered as he drove. "Someone high up in our organization. There are only four or five people who know where the factory is. We got a rat."

Kate listened and said nothing. They got to Quik Nail and parked in the back. Just as they were getting out of the car, Joey Buttons came out of the back door of the nail salon.

"Everyone inside?" Sonny asked.

Instead of answering, Joey held up a meaty hand. "This is as far as you go, Sonny."

Kate's father stopped.

"You ain't invited," said Joey.

"What are you talking about?" Sonny sputtered. "Who says?"

"Benny."

It took a moment for the implications to sink in. "You're gonna let that meathead handle this?" Kate's father asked. "I got more brains in my little finger than he's got in his whole body."

"Benny says it ain't about brains," said Joey.

"Oh, really?" Sonny said. "So what does the great and wise Benny Hacksaw say it's about?"

"Muscle," said Joey. "Benny says someone's gotta stand up to Joe Blattaria. And it ain't you."

"So Benny's decided the Blattarias are behind the hit on the factory?" Sonny asked. "Did he say why he thinks that? Does he have any proof?"

Joey Buttons didn't answer.

"You start a war over this and a lot of people are gonna get hurt," Kate's father warned.

Joey still didn't answer. He crossed his arms and blocked the door.

"Let me ask you something, Joey," Sonny said. "If Benny's so tough, how come he isn't letting me in? What's he afraid of?"

Joey remained tight-lipped, but his forehead creased slightly as if he realized this was an apt question.

Sonny inched closer. "Joey, listen to me. The best thing you could do right now is step out of the way. Benny doesn't know which end of a cow gets milked, much less what to do in a situation like this. There are a lot ways to show strength. But most of the time the most obvious one is the wrong one."

Joey Buttons's eyes darted right and left uncertainly as if he wasn't sure what to do.

"Come on, Joey," Sonny said. "How long you been with me?"

"Twelve years."

"And in all that time, did I ever do you wrong?" Sonny asked.

Joey shook his head.

"Did I always make sure you had money in your pocket?"

Joey nodded.

"So why all of a sudden do you want to listen to that idiot Benny instead of me?" Sonny asked.

"Because Benny says—"

Sonny cut him short. "Talk is cheap, Joey. You want to see how cheap it is? Just let me in that door and I'll show you." Without waiting for an answer, he started to move past Joey. Kate had to admire how persuasive and convincing her father could be. Sonny was just about to reach for the door when it suddenly swung open and Benny Hacksaw stood there.

"What the hell?" Benny growled when he saw Sonny. He spun on Joey Buttons. "I thought I told you not to let him in."

"Yeah, but . . . ," Joey stammered.

"Maybe he knows who to listen to," Sonny said.

"From now on he's listening to me," Benny snarled.

"Who gave you the high-and-mighty power?" Sonny asked.

Benny jabbed his thumb at his own chest. "I gave it to me, okay? 'Cause it's time this gang was run like a gang and not like a frickin' girls' softball team."

"Suppose we ask the crew who they want to lead them?" Sonny suggested, and took another step toward the door.

Benny blocked his path and reached into his jacket as if threatening to pull something out. Kate felt an involuntary gasp catch in her throat.

Sonny stopped. "You gotta be kidding me."

"I'd hate to make a mess out here in the parking lot," Benny growled. "So if I was you, I'd get back in your car and find a girls' softball team to coach."

Sonny didn't budge. "If I coached a girls' softball team, they'd be winners. Which is more than I can say for you."

Benny slowly began to draw his hand out of his jacket. "Move it!"

Sonny headed back to the car, with Kate following. Kate was stunned by what had just happened. It looked like Benny had finally succeeded in his longtime goal of taking control of her father's organization. When Kate saw her father reach for the car door, she automatically headed over to the passenger side.

"Wait," Sonny said.

Kate looked across the hood at him.

"I gotta go somewhere," Sonny said. "And I have to get there fast. You can't come. I'm sorry."

"How am I going to get home?" Kate asked.

"Can you call someone?"

Kate frowned.

"Come on, kid. You saw what just happened," Sonny said. "You know what this means to our family. It's an emergency, Kate. I gotta go speak to certain people, right now."

Kate nodded. "I understand, Dad. Go ahead. I'll find a way home."

"Thanks, kid." Sonny got in the car and took off.

Kate took out her cell phone, thinking she could try Randi or Teddy, but then she changed her mind . . . and called Nick.

They agreed to meet a few blocks away, in the parking lot of a 7-Eleven. Kate walked. By the time she got there she could hear the high-pitched whine of a motorcycle growing louder. The sun was bright and glaring so she stood in the shade of the building. A moment later Nick pulled up on the bright yellow motorcycle. Sunlight glinted off the chrome. He was wearing jeans and a tight blue T-shirt. Sliding off the yellow helmet, he shook out his black hair. Kate couldn't help noticing the muscles under the shirt and the sexy way his hair fell into his blue eyes.

"Surprise, surprise," he said, wiping a few drops of sweat off his forehead. "I sure didn't expect to see your number pop up on my cell."

"It's business," Kate said.

"What's going on?" Nick asked.

"I need you to tell me the truth about something," Kate said.

"Okay."

"Something that happened last night," Kate said. "You know anything about it?"

"Like what?" Nick asked. "What happened?"

Kate raised an eyebrow.

"I don't know what you're talking about," Nick said. "We were all at the cookout last night. What happened?"

Was he telling the truth? Kate wondered. *Or was he that good at lying?*

"All I can tell you is that something bad happened to my father's organization," Kate said. "Certain people think that your people are responsible. I don't know if they're right or wrong. All I know is, they're dead set on making sure someone pays, if you know what I mean."

Nick looked down the street toward Quik Nail in a way that made Kate wonder if he knew where her father's crew was meeting at that very second. He started to put his helmet back on. "Okay, thanks for the tip," he said. "I better go."

"Wait," Kate said. "I also need a favor."

Nick paused with his hands holding the helmet over his head. "Like what?"

"A ride home."

He cocked his head and squinted suspiciously.

"It's not a trick," Kate assured him.

"You sure?" Nick asked.

"I've always been straight with you, Nick," Kate said. "Which is more than I've gotten in return."

"Okay." Nick handed her the spare helmet and patted the seat behind him.

Kate straddled the seat and slid her arms around Nick's waist.

His stomach muscles were taut and hard. The motorcycle's engine revved and Kate pressed her cheek against Nick's back and held on.

She wondered if he drove fast just to get her to squeeze him tight and press herself against him. There was something positively arousing about being on the bike and holding on to Nick, and Kate couldn't help thinking back to the night they spent together in Atlantic City. How sweet and considerate he'd been. How sensitive and sexy. But at the same time there was an aura of dangerousness about him. And familiarity. Both of which she found alluring.

If he could only keep his pants on around other women . . .

It felt like they got to the driveway gate much too soon. Kate didn't want to let go of him, and when she finally did, Nick gave her a sly, knowing smile as if he knew what she was feeling. Kate felt her face flush. She realized that she wanted him to ask to see her again, and she was disappointed when all he said was "Later." Then he turned the motorcycle around and roared off.

Kate started to key in the security code to open the gate, but before she could finish, a car pulled up behind her. It was Teddy. *What was he doing there?*

Teddy leaned his elbow on the car door and scowled at her. "Who was that?"

"Sorry?" Kate said.

"On the motorcycle." Teddy nodded toward the road.

"I . . . I don't know," Kate replied.

Teddy's eyebrows dipped for a second and Kate wondered

if it was possible that he'd actually seen her get off the bike or speak to Nick. If so, then he knew she was lying to him. That felt bad. He didn't deserve it. He'd always been so good to her. And the last thing she wanted to do was lose him. She forced a cheerful smile onto her face. "So to what do I owe this *surprise* visit?"

"Sonny Junior didn't tell you?" Teddy said, looking a bit surprised himself.

As if on cue, the gate opened. Kate instantly knew that her brother must have opened it from inside the house. Teddy reached across the front seat of the Aston Martin and pushed open the passenger door. "Want a ride up the driveway?"

"Sure." Kate got in and they rode toward the house.

When they got there, Sonny Jr. was waiting, wearing a white T-shirt, gray shorts, and sneakers.

"What's going on?" Kate asked.

"Teddy's taking me over to his club to meet the caddy master," Sonny Jr. said.

Kate looked at her brother in disbelief. "You're going to be a caddy?"

"Teddy says I can make some major bucks," Sonny Jr. said. "Plus it's outside and good exercise."

Kate watched her brother get into the Aston Martin. Tears of gratitude threatened to spill out of her eyes. Teddy was so good to her. How could she lie to him?

"Oh, there's one other thing," Teddy said. "What we talked about at the club."

Kate frowned. There was so much going on that it was hard to remember what he was talking about.

"About Twelve Mile Island?" Teddy prompted her.

"Oh, right. I'm sorry, Teddy, I've got so much on my mind. Can we talk about it later?"

"If you miss Momma's Italian ice with frozen custard you'll never forgive yourself," Teddy said.

"I believe you, Teddy," Kate said. "Really, I do. I just need some time, okay?"

"Sure," Teddy said. "Call you later?"

"Definitely."

Teddy and Sonny Jr. left. Kate let herself into the house. Going to the beach with Teddy was tempting, but how could she leave when her father was in such a crisis? Besides, Teddy's parents, or at least his mother, would be at the beach. Kate wasn't sure she could deal with that kind of disapproval.

No sooner had she gotten up to her room than her cell phone rang. It was Randi.

"Hey," Kate answered.

"What's up?" Randi asked.

Kate told her about Teddy's arranging for Sonny Jr. to get a summer job at the Eagle Crest club. "I swear, Randi, I don't know what I did to deserve such a nice guy."

"You're a great person, Kate. Why shouldn't you deserve him?"

The image of Nick Blattaria on his motorcycle roared into her head. Nick with his tight T-shirt and firm muscles and confident, knowing smile. He was the reason Kate didn't deserve someone as nice as Teddy.

"He wants me to come to his beach house," Kate said.

"Nice," Randi said. "Where is it?"

"Fair Haven," Kate said. "On Twelve Mile Island."

"Sounds great. I mean—omigod!"

"What?" Kate asked.

"Isn't Fair Haven the town next to Oceandale?" Randi said.

"So?"

"Oceandale's where Wendy Williams's parents have their beach house."

"And your point is?"

"I have this revenge fantasy," Randi said. "It's like the best thing ever. Does Teddy's beach house have a pool?"

"I don't know. I guess it would."

"Oh, this is just too perfect!"

17

ROUND DINNERTIME KATE WAS IN HER ROOM WHEN she heard a car come up the driveway, and then voices outside. She looked out the window. Teddy's Aston Martin was parked out front.

She got downstairs just as Sonny Jr. came in wearing a blue bib with the blue-and-gold Eagle Crest logo on it.

"How'd it go?" she asked.

"Great!" Sonny Jr. answered with a youthful excitement Kate hadn't seen from him in a long time. "I'm gonna make a ton of money! The other caddies are cool. They say you can really get buff carrying the bags around the course."

"Where's Teddy?" Kate asked.

"He just left," said Sonny Jr..

Left? Kate hurried out the front door. The Aston Martin was halfway down the driveway. "Teddy!" she called, jogging after the car.

The car came to a stop and Teddy twisted his head around and smiled. "Hey."

"Why didn't you come in?" Kate asked.

"You seemed like you had a lot on your mind before," Teddy said. "I didn't want to put anything more on your plate."

"Listen, I don't know how I can thank you for what you did for my brother."

"You could agree to go to the beach next week," Teddy said.

Kate pursed her lips with frustration. She did want to go to the beach with him, but the idea of leaving her father, and of seeing Teddy's parents again, completely turned her off. As usual, Teddy had the ability to read her thoughts.

"Blessing, listen," he said. "I know my parents gave you a hard time at the club last winter, but try to see it from their point of view. You weren't what they were expecting. That doesn't mean they won't come around. You know how sometimes you hear a song and the first time it doesn't do anything for you, but after you've heard it a few times it can really grow on you? That's what it's like with my parents."

Kate gave him a bittersweet smile. "I'm just not sure I want to 'grow' on anyone. Seriously, Teddy, if they don't like me the way I am, why bother?"

"What if I told you I've done the bothering for you?" Teddy asked.

"What do you mean?" Kate asked uncertainly.

"I told them about that you're on the honor roll and about your extracurricular activities and what a great person you are. They know they shouldn't judge you just because your parents didn't go to college."

That might have been true, but Kate couldn't help but wonder how Teddy's parents would feel if they knew what her father really did for a living. Teddy drummed his fingers against the car's polished wood steering wheel. Kate could tell he really wanted her to come to the beach, and she felt bad because she also wanted to go. She just worried that it would be a decision she'd come to regret.

"Blessing, can I trust you not to repeat something to anyone?" Teddy asked.

If only he knew what I already can't repeat, she thought. "Yes, Teddy."

"My family isn't so perfect," he said. "Back in the eighties my grandfather was charged with stock manipulation and insider trading. He had to pay a huge fine and was banned from the investment business for two years. We laugh about it now and call it 'Grandpa's Mistake,' but everyone knows it was no mistake. He knew exactly what he was doing."

Kate imagined it had taken a lot for Teddy to tell her that. She could see how hard he was trying to get her to change her mind. At any other time she would have relented and agreed to go to the beach. But she didn't want to leave her father right now.

She leaned over the side of the car and kissed him lightly on the lips. "I appreciate what you're trying to do, Teddy. Really, I do. But I'm just not up to it right now. I'd really love to see you when you get back, okay? Can we make plans?"

Teddy looked away and hung his head slightly. Kate wondered if he was gathering his strength for another attempt at getting her to go. Instead he nodded slowly. "Okay, I hear you. I'm around until noon tomorrow. If you change your mind between now and then, I'd love to hear from you. Otherwise, as soon as I get back, I'll call."

Feeling a pang of regret, Kate watched him drive away. How many more times could she disappoint him? How many more times could she lie to him before he'd finally decide he'd had enough?

That night Kate hardly got any sleep. There were so many problems and uncertainties in her life. Would her mother ever come home? Would her father be able to regain control of his organization from Uncle Benny? Why couldn't she let go of Nick Blattaria? And just how long would it be before Teddy said good riddance once and for all?

The next morning Kate made herself a cappuccino and carried it out to the pool. Sitting at the outdoor table she took a deep breath of the cool air. It was before seven a.m. and the air still had a moist coolness that would soon disappear. Kate yawned. She felt bleary. She doubted she'd gotten more than four hours of sleep.

The sliding doors opened and her father came out looking haggard. Kate could tell he'd been up all night. His jaw was covered with dark stubble and his normally neat clothes were wrinkled and disheveled, the tails of his shirt untucked. As he slumped down into the chair across from her, Kate noticed something jutting against his shirt near his waist. For a second she couldn't believe what she was seeing. He was carrying. Now she knew why his shirttails were out. This was the first time she'd ever seen her father with a gun.

Meanwhile, Sonny focused on the cup of cappuccino. "May I?"

"Be my guest," Kate said.

Her father picked up the cup and took a sip. "Good."

"Thanks, Dad. How's it going?"

Sonny shook his head grimly. "Not good."

"Anything I can do?" Kate asked.

Her father looked up and straight into her eyes. "Yeah, I need you and Sonny Junior to go away for a few days."

The suggestion surprised Kate. "Why?"

"Because it could be dangerous for you here," Sonny said.

"Dad, I can deal," Kate said.

"No arguments, kid," her father said firmly. "This is the way it's going to be. You're out of here till I say it's safe to come back. I've already spoken to your mother. She's got room on her couch for one of you, and I figure that has to be Sonny Junior because he's got nowhere else to go. You've got plenty of friends, so find one who won't ask questions, okay?"

"When do I have to go?" Kate asked.

"Now."

"Dad, it's not even seven o'clock in the morning," Kate said. "I can't call anyone now."

"Then as soon as you can," Sonny said.

Birds chirped in the trees. The pool was glassy. Everything was quiet and peaceful at this hour. *The calm before the storm,* Kate thought.

"Dad?" Kate said.

"Hmmm?"

"I've never seen you carrying before," Kate said.

Sonny smirked and pulled his shirt down. "It's been a while. Guess I'm not so good at it, huh?"

"Is it really that bad?" Kate asked.

"Benny's declared an all-out war," Sonny said. "Willy Shoes almost got his head shot off last night in a drive-by. Can you imagine? Willy, of all the guys. He'll probably spend the next month hiding under his bed."

"You're sure it was the Blattarias who hit the factory?" Kate asked.

"Who else?" asked her father.

"Dad, without the factory, can we even afford to live here anymore?" Kate asked.

Her father gazed up at the sky. A dragonfly hovered briefly over the pool, then flitted away. Sonny said, "I hate to say it, Kate, but this could be the end for us. I mean, we'll work something out. We'll live somewhere, but it's gonna be different."

Different meant less well-off. No big house with an indoor-outdoor pool. No Mercedes Benz for her. No wads of cash to blow on clothes at the mall. She felt her heart sink. She'd taken so much for granted, never pausing for a moment to think of how shaky their life was. It was all based on crime, for God's sake. How could she have been so foolish as to think it would just go on forever? And yet she had, in part because her parents had wanted it that way. But maybe this was part of growing up—realizing how quickly it could all be taken away.

She waited until nine and then called Randi.

"Hope I didn't wake you," Kate said when her friend answered the phone.

"Are you kidding?" Randi groaned. "My five-year-old twin cousins are here from Ohio. They've been up since six this morning and so has everyone else. So what's up?"

"I guess with your cousins there you wouldn't have a place for me to stay for a few days, huh?" Kate said.

"Why? What's going on?"

"Uh, we're having the floors done," Kate lied. "They put down that polyurethane and it's such a yucky smell."

"The worst," Randi agreed. "Only, like I said, my aunt and uncle are staying here with their kids. They're in my room and I'm on the couch in the den. There's hardly even room for me. Is there anyone else you can try? What about Teddy? Didn't he invite you to his beach house for the week?"

"Uh-huh."

"Have you lost your mind?" Randi asked. "You have a choice between staying in my hot little house in town or his mansion on the beach and you called me first?"

"It's not that simple," Kate said. "His mother will be there and his father will come for the weekend."

"So?"

"So they don't approve of me," Kate said. "Not only that, but they don't mind letting me know that they don't approve of me."

"Then tell Teddy you don't want to spend any time with them."

"It's hard to avoid them when you're a guest in their house."

"A small price to pay when it means being at the beach," Randi said.

"I don't know," said Kate.

"Look at it this way. You already know they don't like you, so it won't be any worse than you imagine. And once they get to know you, it'll probably get better."

There was a strange logic to that. It probably couldn't be any worse than she imagined, and at least she'd be at the beach.

"I guess you're right," Kate said.

"And don't forget my revenge fantasy."

"Sure, Randi, I won't forget."

"Seriously?" Randi said. "If you go, promise you'll call me, okay?"

Kate promised she would. She hung up and dialed Teddy's number. She couldn't blame him for sounding a little bit surprised to hear from her.

"I'll get right to the point," Kate said. "Am I still invited to the beach?"

18

AN HOUR LATER TEDDY PULLED UP IN FRONT OF THE house. Kate could tell he was delighted that she'd changed her mind, though too polite to ask why. They drove to the shore with the top down and the radio on. At first Kate felt guilty about leaving her father with so many problems, but it was his decision that she should go, not hers. Besides, now that people were shooting at one another she had to wonder what good she could possibly be. Sonny was probably right. She was better off leaving him with one less person to worry about. Of course, she'd have to call him every night and make sure he was okay.

She glanced across the seat at Teddy, who drove with the sun on his shoulders and a smile on his face. He grinned at her, but she couldn't help wondering if he would be as happy if he knew that her family was currently involved in an underworld gang war. Maybe it was true that his grandfather had once gotten in trouble for doing something wrong in the stock market, but there was a big difference between Wall Street and street war.

They drove over the Twelve Mile Island causeway above a wide, glistening bay. A few sailboats were out, their sails bulging tight, and seagulls floated on the breeze overhead. On the other side of the causeway the island stretched long and narrow with one main road running its length. This street was lined with restaurants, T-shirt, ice cream, and surf shops, seafood stores, and motels. The air smelled salty, and at stoplights families armed with beach chairs, umbrellas, and body boards crossed the road on their way to the beach.

"Surf's up," Teddy said.

"How can you tell?"

He pointed at the side of the road where a bare-chested kid with long sun-bleached hair steered a bike with one hand and carried a short white surfboard under his other arm.

"You surf?" Kate asked.

"Oh, yeah." Teddy answered in a way that sounded like he couldn't wait to get into the waves. Kate had never thought of him as the surfer type, but by now she knew she shouldn't be surprised by anything she learned about Teddy.

They passed block after block of beach houses. The farther they got from the causeway, the larger the beach houses became, until there were no longer blocks of houses, but houses on pieces of property the size of blocks.

Finally Teddy slowed and turned through an open gate in a tall green hedge clearly designed for privacy. A sign beside the gate warned against trespassing. As they drove up the tree-lined drive, Kate knew the house would be spectacular, but what she hadn't anticipated was the pool and tennis court they passed first, both set among trees and sharing a single large cabana. The house itself was a soft white, vast and low, as if designed to fit among the dunes. It had broad greenish-blue windows and a wide wooden deck with lounges and a hot tub. To the right, nestled behind some trees, was a separate four-car garage. Teddy opened the Aston Martin's glove compartment and fumbled through the garage door openers inside for the right one.

"Ah, so many garage door openers and so little time," Kate teased.

"I think it's ridiculous that my parents seem to need three different houses," Teddy said. "But that's never stopped me from enjoying them."

He found the right remote and they drove into the garage, where a gorgeous silver sports car, a classic Mercedes-Benz, was already parked.

"Mom's here," Teddy said when he saw it. "Down here at the beach we try to keep the cars protected. Otherwise the sun and salt air does a number on them."

From the garage they walked along a breezeway lined with screens. Kate could hear the steady crash of the waves.

"I love that sound," she said.

"Me, too," said Teddy. "We'll get out there in a second, but first I want to show you your room."

The side of the house that faced the ocean was almost all glass, and Kate could see the white beach dotted here and there with colorful umbrellas. Beyond that were the blue-green waves.

Several large sailboats with billowing white sails cut across the horizon.

"Here you go," Teddy said, holding open a door for her.

Kate stepped into a bedroom with a king-size bed and a huge armoire with a television inside. On the far side of the room were large windows and a sliding glass door covered by gauzy white curtains. Kate put down her bag and pulled back the curtains to enjoy the view of the beach.

"I'll leave you here to change," Teddy said. "When you're ready, just go out the sliding door. I'll be on the deck with Mom."

Teddy left, but Kate didn't move from the windows. Outside was the deck, and while she couldn't see Mrs. Fitzgerald, she knew she was there. Having to say hello to Teddy's mother before going to the beach was sort of like having to take some huge test before getting to go on vacation. Oh, well... She sighed. At least she had the beach to look forward to.

Kate had brought both a two-piece and a one-piece bathing suit. The one-piece was for when Teddy's parents were around, so she put that one on. It was aqua blue with green trim and green shoulder straps. In the mirror-lined bathroom she brushed her hair and put on sunscreen. Finally, feeling a nervous, fluttering sensation in her stomach, Kate slid open the glass door and stepped out onto the deck. Instantly the roar of the waves was in her ears and the salt air in her nostrils. To her left were some lounge chairs. Mrs. Fitzgerald was sitting in one, facing the ocean. She was wearing sunglasses, a green bathing suit with gold piping, and a wide-brimmed white hat. On a small table beside her was a book, and a tall glass containing some kind of drink with ice and a wedge of lime. Teddy was sitting on the lounge next to hers, wearing the same blue Hawaiian board shorts he'd worn at Kate's New Year's Eve party.

Mrs. Fitzgerald turned her head toward Kate. It was impossible to see her eyes behind the sunglasses. "Hello, dear. How nice of you to come."

"Thanks for having me," Kate said.

"Our pleasure," replied Mrs. Fitzgerald. "Teddy always enjoys having friends visit so that he doesn't have to spend time with his father and me."

"You should be glad, Mom," Teddy said. "I'd be worried if I had a seventeen-year-old son who'd rather hang out with his parents than his friends."

"I suppose you're right," Mrs. Fitzgerald said. "Well, go on, have fun."

Teddy led Kate down some wooden steps.

"Was that so bad?" he whispered.

"Not at all."

"I'm telling you, they understand that you can't be held responsible for your parents' actions."

Kate smiled appreciatively. She wondered what Teddy would think if he knew that for the past seven months she'd been as responsible for running her father's organization as her father had, and that the chief reason for her coming to the beach was to make sure she was out of danger when the bullets started flying. Would he still like her this much? Was she deceiving him by not telling him the truth? Wouldn't she have to tell him someday?

At the bottom of the steps, Teddy looked out at the waves. "How about some body boarding?"

"Great," said Kate.

He led her under the deck to a storage room filled with surf-boards, body boards, kayaks, beach chairs, and assorted other beach gear. There was so much equipment that Kate joked, "Do you run a camp here?"

"Lots of relatives," Teddy said. "Various members of the Fitzgerald clan spend a few weeks here each summer. Sometimes there's more than a dozen of them."

Kate noticed he was looking at her feet. "Is there something wrong with them?" she asked.

Teddy laughed. "No, I was just gauging what size flippers you'll need."

"Why flippers?" Kate asked.

"You'll see," Teddy said.

They each took a body board and a pair of stubby flippers and headed down to the water. Teddy was already on his way to a caramel tan. Kate was reminded of the kid they'd seen on the bike earlier with the surfboard under his arm. Five years ago Teddy probably looked just like that—skinny and wiry, with long sun-bleached hair. Now he was taller and more muscular, and his hair was shorter and a slightly darker shade of blond.

At the ocean's edge Teddy showed her how to put on the flip-pers and back into the waves until she was deep enough to turn around and start swimming. Out beyond the surf he showed her how to use the flippers to catch a wave and ride sideways like a surfer. It seemed like they stayed in the water for hours.

Finally they got out and sat on the beach, catching their breaths. The sun's rays warmed Kate's chilled skin.

"Fun, huh?" Teddy said.

Kate nodded. Sea water dripped from her hair.

"I could stay in the water all day," he said.

"Don't let me stop you," Kate said.

Teddy gazed out at the waves. Kate glanced up and down the beach. A quarter of a mile in both directions were crowds of people and umbrellas and a couple of bright orange lifeguard stands. But where Teddy and she sat, there was hardly anyone. Just one family with a beach umbrella in one direction and a couple of chubby men with cigars sitting in beach chairs in the other.

"How come it's so crowded over there and not here?" she asked.

"That's the public beach," Teddy said.

"This isn't public?" Kate asked.

"Well, technically it is," Teddy said. "Anyone from the public beach can walk over here and sit if they want."

"Why don't they?" Kate asked.

"I don't know. I guess they don't feel a need to. Hey, look." He pointed out past the waves.

At first Kate didn't know what he was pointing at. Then she saw a dark, triangular fin break the surface for a second before disappearing into the water again.

"Shark!?" she gasped.

"Porpoise," Teddy said. "They swim up and down the shore

looking for bait fish. Sometimes when you're out there you can almost get close enough to touch them."

The porpoises swam past, their backs rising and disappearing again and again until they were no longer visible. Kate liked the side of Teddy that enjoyed the sight of porpoises frolicking, and that wanted to help kids like her brother stay out of trouble.

After a while they went back into the water for another body boarding session, then walked up the beach and rinsed off under an outdoor shower. Back on the deck, with the sun starting its downward path in the western part of the sky, Teddy brought out lemonade and a bowl of fruit.

Kate took of sip of the lemonade. It was freshly squeezed, not frozen or from a container. She couldn't imagine Teddy's mother making it herself. Kate looked toward the kitchen, where a small woman in a white uniform was drying glasses by hand.

"Where's your mom?" Kate asked.

"She usually plays golf or tennis in the afternoons," Teddy said.

Kate heard the *pock* of a tennis ball coming from the court on the inland side of the house.

"You can tell me if this is none of my business," Teddy said, "but what made you change your mind about coming?"

Kate's first inclination was to lie and say that she'd had a change of heart. But she caught herself. What was the point? If she was going to have any kind of a future with Teddy, wouldn't he have to learn the truth sooner or later?

"Teddy, the reason I didn't come in the first place is because my dad's having business problems and I thought if I stayed around I could help," she said. "The reason I changed my mind is because he doesn't want me around right now . . . because it might be dangerous for me."

Teddy shook his head slowly, as if in amazement.

"In case you're wondering," Kate continued, "I don't plan on doing this my whole life. I mean, after college I'm definitely going into the legitimate side of business. But right now I have to do what's best for my family. You can understand, can't you?"

Teddy widened his eyes slowly, and then nodded. Kate interpreted the gesture to mean that he understood, but at the same time, she'd have to admit that it was fairly unusual, wouldn't she?

"This is who I am, Teddy," Kate said. She didn't have to add *Take it or leave it.*

Teddy looked at his watch. "We should get dressed. We're sort of required to have dinner with my parents tonight. Tomorrow night we're on our own."

Back in the guest bedroom Kate was beginning to feel tired. She'd hardly gotten any sleep the night before and the bed looked incredibly inviting, but it didn't sound like there'd be time for a nap. Then she noticed a message on her cell phone. It was from Randi. Kate called her back.

"You promised you'd call," Randi said when she answered the phone.

"This was my first chance," Kate said with a yawn.

"How's it going?"

"Okay, I guess." Kate thought about the conversation she and

Teddy had just had. She still wasn't certain how he'd reacted to what she'd told him. "How about you?"

"Just a blast," Randi said with a groan. "It's about a million degrees out, so we're all stuck in the house with the air-conditioning and one of the twins just threw up on the carpet in my room. So what's it like there?"

"It's nice," Kate said, not wanting to tell her too much for fear of making her even more miserable.

"Yeah, right. I'll bet it's nice," Randi guffawed. "I'm looking at a Twelve Mile Island beach cam on my computer right now. It's gorgeous. I bet if I ask how Teddy's house is, you'll say quaint."

Kate glanced around the guest bedroom. This house was nothing short of magnificent. "Listen, Randi, can you blame me for not wanting to tell you how nice it is? All it'll do is make you feel bad."

"You want me to feel good? Get Teddy to invite Tanner and Stu over for a swim."

"There's no way he's going to do that."

"Why not?" Randi asked. "They're teammates."

"But not really friends."

"So? You invited them to your New Year's Eve party."

"We've always invited the whole grade," Kate said. "It's a tradition."

"Then make a new tradition."

"Randi, I'm just a guest myself," Kate argued. "I can't ask him to invite over other people."

"Do I have to remind you of something spelled, B-R-I-N-K-S?"

Randi said. "Or how about our new venture? And all the promises you made to me on your pink My Little Pony? I mean, you owe me so much..."

She was right. Without her help, life these last seven months would have been much different. The Brink's holdup had yielded roughly a million dollars, all thanks to Randi. And probably the only chance left for her father's organization was in Randi's "new venture" hands.

"You're right," Kate said. "I'm sorry I even gave you a hard time about it. I owe you big-time."

"Come through for me on this and we'll be even," Randi said.

"I'll do what I can," Kate promised.

"Attagirl," Randi said. "One thing I know about you, when you put your mind to something, you always succeed."

Kate hung up. Randi's plan was nothing short of outrageous. Kate couldn't imagine Teddy ever agreeing to it. But for Randi's sake, she had to try.

19

KATE SHOWERED AND DRESSED FOR DINNER. SHE chose a white sundress and an aqua summer shawl in case the restaurant was air-conditioned to a chill. She and Teddy rode in his car to the restaurant. As Teddy followed his father's Bentley, Kate was surprised by how nervous she felt. Given the fact that back home she was dealing with a gang war and an FBI investigation, she wouldn't have thought that dinner with Teddy's folks would raise her pulse.

At dinner, much to Kate's relief, Teddy's parents were civil and friendly. They ate on a terrace overlooking the bay and watched the sun go down. Not a word was breathed about Kate's parents. Mr. Fitzgerald talked mostly about the All-England Tennis Championships at Wimbledon and the PGA tour. Mrs. Fitzgerald channeled her comments toward ladies' golf and shopping. Still, Kate was so tense she hardly touched her lobster and fresh corn on the cob.

When dinner ended Kate felt nothing but relief. Outside, they waited for the valet parking attendants to get their cars. It was dark, and moths darted madly under the lights.

Teddy's mother took Kate's hand in hers. "It's so good to see you again. We're so delighted you could come to the shore."

Kate thanked her, but she felt the oddest sensation. As if Mrs. Fitzgerald knew something she and Teddy didn't know. Kate decided it was just her overactive imagination.

She kept a smile on her face and waved as Teddy's parents drove away.

"Thank God that's over," Teddy said with a wink. The parking attendant brought the Aston Martin around and Kate got in.

"You must be starved," Teddy said as they drove away. "You hardly touched your dinner."

Once again Kate marveled at how observant he was. "I'm still too nervous to be hungry."

"Well, you've been through the worst of it," he said.

To Kate it still felt a little strange. Almost as if she had to get his parents' approval before she and Teddy could proceed any further. Oh, well, maybe that was just how really rich people did things.

As they drove through the cool evening air, Kate began to relax. The knot in her stomach began to loosen into hunger pangs. They turned onto the main street and found themselves in a long line of traffic.

"Welcome to Friday night on Twelve Mile Island," Teddy said. "The world's longest parking lot. The good news is, we're just a few blocks away from heaven."

Momma's was an old wooden shack with sliding windows where servers took orders. Next to it was a miniature golf course. A line of people stretched off the raised deck and two dozen yards down the block—mostly parents and kids, but here and there a pocket of teenagers. With a start Kate noticed a couple of the guys with popped-up collars near the front of the line. Stu and Tanner were standing there with the BMWs. It would have been an amazing coincidence, except that practically everyone went to Momma's after dinner.

"Teddy?" she said quietly.

Teddy gave her a puzzled look, clearly wondering why she'd lowered her voice.

"I need to ask you a huge favor," Kate said. "Is your pool heated?"

"No, why?" Teddy said.

"How's the water right now?" Kate asked.

"I don't follow," said Teddy.

"Is it warm, or still kind of cool?"

"Kind of cool, actually," Teddy said. "It doesn't usually warm up until the end of July. Why?"

"I'll tell you in a second," Kate said. "Just one more question. Is your house wired for WiFi?"

Teddy nodded. Kate whispered in his ear for a long time. When she was finished, he backed away and stared at her with astonishment.

"I made a promise," Kate said. "And think of what they did to Randi." She didn't bother to add that this past winter, after she and Tanner broke up, he'd spread awful rumors about her on the Internet. So she had her own motive for revenge.

"Two wrongs don't make a right," Teddy said.

"An eye for an eye," countered Kate.

One of Teddy's eyebrows dipped, and she knew he was considering it. He shuddered. "Why do I get the feeling I should never cross you?"

Kate threw her arms around his neck. "Thank you!"

They stood in line and waited. At the order windows, Stu, Tanner, and the BMWs got their custard and ices and left. In a moment they would pass Teddy and Kate. Kate was worried that Teddy might change his mind, but just as Stu and Tanner passed them he reached out and gave Tanner a light tap on the shoulder.

Tanner looked surprised to see him and Kate, but then he grinned. "Hey, bro, what's up?"

"Not much," Teddy replied smoothly. "You?"

"Just chillin'," Tanner said, his eyes darting to Kate.

The BMWs joined them. It was obvious they'd spent the day in the sun. Brandy and Mandy were a medium shade of pink while Wendy was as red as a lobster. The three girls focused on Kate.

"Staying with Teddy?" Brandy asked.

Kate nodded.

Brandy bit her lip and her eyes darted to Teddy. Kate suspected she was dying to ask what Teddy's house was like, but couldn't with Teddy there.

"Good waves today, huh?" Teddy asked.

Stu made a face. "They sure *looked* good. Only you're not allowed to surf at the public beach, so all we could do was watch them."

"Why don't you come over to my place tomorrow afternoon?" Teddy suggested. "Around two, when the tide's right. We could surf and then take a swim in the pool."

Stu and Tanner and the BMWs shared a surprised look that quickly became eager agreement. They thanked Teddy and then took off to hear a band. Kate and Teddy stayed on line.

"What do your parents usually do in the morning?" Kate asked.

"Golf," Teddy said.

"What about you?" Kate asked.

"I have a feeling I'll be making myself scarce for a few hours," Teddy said.

Kate grinned and kissed him.

They got ices with custard and played miniature golf. When they finished with tie scores, Kate suspected that Teddy had missed a few shots on purpose. By then it was getting late and Kate was tired.

"This was fun," she said with a yawn.

"Time for you to go to bed," Teddy said.

"No, no," Kate protested. "I'll stay up if you want to do something."

"I'm ready to turn in," Teddy said.

Kate remembered getting into Teddy's car, but the next thing she knew, they were back at the beach house, parked in the driveway. Overhead the black sky glittered with stars.

"What happened?" Kate asked with a yawn.

"You fell asleep the moment your head hit the headrest," Teddy said. "I thought I was going to have to carry you inside."

Kate smiled dreamily and looked up at the star-washed sky. "It's so beautiful here."

"You should see it in August during the Perseids."

"The what?" Kate said.

"The annual meteor shower that peaks around mid-August," Teddy explained. "It's called the Perseids because it comes from a part of the sky where the constellation Perseus is. If you get a clear night it's the most amazing thing to see." He leaned slightly closer. "Maybe you'll come back to see it."

"I'd like that," Kate said, then yawned again. "Sorry."

Teddy chuckled. "Come on, let's get you to bed."

He walked her to the guest room. She stopped at the door and turned to him. "Thanks for a fun day and night."

"My pleasure." He kissed her briefly on the lips. "I'll get going early in the morning and be back around eleven. Will that work?"

"Perfectly," Kate said.

In the guest bedroom, Kate couldn't wait to lay her head on the pillow. But first she had to call Randi. "Okay," she said when Randi answered. "You've got the green light. They're coming at two o' clock, so you have to make sure everything is set up by then."

"You guys are the best!" Randi squealed over the phone. "Give Teddy a big kiss for me."

"I will," Kate said. "When the time's right."

20

I N THE MORNING WHEN KATE WOKE, THE HOUSE WAS EMPTY.
Or so she thought. Wandering into the kitchen, she discovered the woman in the white uniform polishing a silver bowl.
Her name was Carmen, and she gestured for Kate to sit outside
on the deck at a table under an umbrella.

Kate sat down. The sky was blue and the air was already
warm. A quarter-mile down the beach in both directions at the
public beaches people had already started to put up umbrellas.
Carmen brought out a small tray with coffee, cream, and a bowl
of fresh fruit.

Kate had to admit that this was the most beautiful spot for a
breakfast that she'd ever seen. Except for a lady walking a large
brown dog, the beach in front of the Fitzgeralds' house was
empty. The waves crashed rhythmically and a small band of sand-
pipers scurried along the water's edge, stopping here and there to
poke their long beaks into the sand.

Kate sipped her coffee and picked at the fruit—fresh

strawberries, pineapple, and melon. It was so idyllic, she didn't even mind being alone. She checked her watch. Randi would be there soon.

Carmen returned with a tray with eggs and toast. *Livin' large,* Kate thought.

She'd just finished breakfast when her phone rang. It was Randi.

"Tell me I'm not dreaming," Randi said when Kate answered.

"Where are you?" Kate asked.

"At the gate."

"You're not dreaming," Kate said. "I'll come get you."

Randi was waiting in a green Toyota Corolla.

"Where'd you get this?" Kate asked.

"Our new venture's starting to pay off," Randi answered. "It's going to kill me if the day ever comes when I have to give it up. So what's with all you rich people and these gates? Afraid the proletariat are going to rise up and revolt?"

"I don't think the Fitzgeralds have gates for the same reason we do," Kate said. "Or maybe they do. I haven't asked."

Randi pushed open the passenger door. "Want a ride up the driveway?"

Kate got in and looked into the backseat, which was covered with wires, light fixtures, duct and electrical tape, an electric drill, screwdrivers, and wrenches. A laptop computer in a black case lay on the floor. "You sure you've got everything?" she teased.

"Hey, I've come prepared." Randi said. "This is one golden opportunity."

It took Randi close to two hours to get it all set up and working. Kate was impressed with how thoroughly her friend had thought the plan out, right down to shutting off the hot water valve in the cabana shower.

"Done," Randi finally said, wiping a light patina of sweat off her forehead and gazing longingly at the pool. "I would so love to jump in."

Kate checked her watch. Teddy would be home in about fifteen minutes. "There isn't time. You know the deal. You were never here. Teddy never saw you."

Randi made an unhappy face. "Promise you'll call me as soon as they leave, okay?"

"I promise," Kate said. "But won't you already know?"

"Oh, I'll know all right," Randi said. "I'll just need to gloat."

Randi left, and a little while later Teddy returned. Kate was sitting on the desk when he came out.

"Everything go okay?" he asked.

"I thought you didn't want to know," Kate said.

"You're right." He glanced toward the pool. "So, to the beach?"

They got beach chairs and an umbrella and went down to the water's edge. Were it not for the fact that they were almost completely alone—and that Carmen came down to the beach every half hour to take drink orders—they could have been on any beach anywhere.

Promptly at two p.m. Stu, Tanner, and the BMWs arrived. Stu

and Tanner wore board shorts and carried surfboards. The BMWs wore bikinis and carried matching pink-mesh beach bags.

"This is frickin' awesome!" Tanner gasped, gesturing at the wide expanse of empty beach. "No crowds, no annoying lifeguards. It's perfect!"

"Waves look good too," Stu said.

"Why don't you guys go in," Teddy said, getting to his feet. "I'll get my board."

"Great!" Stu and Tanner headed for the waves and Teddy went back up the beach. The BMWs pulled beach towels out of their bags and spread them on the sand, then sprayed each other with Bain de Soleil suntanning mist.

"Backs or fronts?" Wendy asked.

"Backs," said Mandy.

All three girls lay on their stomachs and tanned their backs. Kate, who sat in the shade of the umbrella, wondered if it was utterly unacceptable for one of them to do anything different from the other two.

"Aren't you going to get tan?" Brandy asked Kate.

"I like to wait until the sun's not quite so strong," Kate answered.

"Why?" asked Wendy.

"Because she doesn't want to get burned," Mandy said. "Duh."

"You can use some of our spray," Wendy offered.

"Thanks, but I've read that they don't really block out all the harmful rays," Kate said.

The BMWs didn't respond. Clearly, for them, the need to get a dark tan outweighed whatever harmful rays were out there.

Teddy trotted past them with a surfboard under his arm. Without stopping, he launched himself into the water, gliding half a dozen yards before starting to paddle. Kate again had a vision of that bare-chested young boy with the sun-streaked hair, riding his bicycle with a board under his arm.

"So what's with you and Teddy?" Brandy asked.

"Just friends," Kate replied.

"Are you sure?" Wendy asked. "I mean, he did invite you to his beach house. Wouldn't that mean something more?"

"I don't think so," Kate replied. "Does it mean more than your inviting Brandy, Mandy, Stu, and Tanner to *your* beach house?"

"You know, Kate, we really all should be friends," Brandy said. "I mean, seriously, what's the point of being enemies? We have so much in common."

Kate didn't respond immediately. She was curious about what Brandy thought they had in common.

"I mean, let's face it," she said. "We have the best clothes and the hottest guys. Imagine what it would be like if we joined forces?"

"What about Randi?" Kate asked.

Another awkward silence followed. "But she's kind of fat," Wendy finally said.

"It's not just that," Mandy added. "It's her whole 'open and honest about sex' thing. It's really not cool."

"She's just being honest," Kate pointed out. "Like she always says, she's not doing anything you guys aren't doing."

"But she doesn't have to be so public about it," Brandy said.

"That's the way she is," Kate said. "There's not a hypocritical bone in her body. I find it kind of refreshing."

The conversation went nowhere after that. While the BMWs might have been willing to allow Kate to join their ranks (would they then be called the BMWKs? she wondered), it was clear that there was no way they were going to open their hearts to Randi. Instead, at the appointed moment, all three rolled onto their backs, dug iPods out of their bags, and plugged in. Kate couldn't help but wonder if they were listening to the same playlist.

The guys stayed in the water for about an hour. When they came out, Kate noticed their lips were blue and their teeth were chattering.

"That water's cold," Stu said with a shiver.

"It's the currents," Teddy said. "Why don't we shower off and change into dry stuff?" After he said this, he glanced at Kate and winked.

"You sure you don't want to sit in the sun for a while and warm up?" Tanner asked.

"If we warm up on the deck we can grab a beer, too," Teddy said.

"Sounds good to me," said Stu.

"Can we jump in the pool?" asked Brandy.

"Sure," said Teddy.

Everyone packed their stuff and headed back up the beach toward the house. "I better warn you that the pool's still pretty cold at this time of year," Teddy said.

"I think I'll skip it and take a shower," said Tanner.

"Me too," said Stu.

"I just want to jump in for a second," said Brandy. "After all that sun, I'm fried."

When they got to the pool, Stu and Tanner went into the cabana to shower while the BMWs jumped in the water. Kate joined them. The water was indeed cold, but refreshing. Rather than shower, Teddy took a seat.

The girls got out of the pool just about the same time Stu and Tanner came out of the cabana. Both of them had towels wrapped over their shoulders. Their lips were blue and their teeth chattering.

"How was the shower?" Teddy asked innocently.

Stu and Tanner shared uncertain looks as if they weren't sure what to say. Finally Tanner spoke: "Hate to say it, dude, but your hot water isn't working."

"You took *cold* showers?" Teddy asked with feigned surprise.

"*Really* cold," Stu said.

Teddy apologized and the group headed for the deck, where Carmen provided snacks and beer and soda. By the time they finished, the afternoon was almost over. Stu, Tanner, and the BMWs thanked Teddy and left.

"Think it worked?" Teddy asked Kate as soon as they were gone.

"Only one way to tell," Kate said. She flipped open her cell phone and called Randi.

The phone rang a few times.

Then someone answered.

But all Kate could hear was screaming.

21

"RANDI?" KATE SAID. "RANDI? IS THAT YOU? ARE YOU OKAY?"

The screaming continued. Kate didn't know what to do.

"What's wrong?" Teddy asked.

"Someone answered and she's screaming," Kate said. "I think it's Randi, but I'm not sure." She handed the phone to Teddy. But even when he pressed it to his ear, Kate could still hear the screams.

"Randi?" Teddy said. "Randi, can you hear me?"

The screaming continued. Teddy handed the phone back to Kate. "Maybe it's a wrong number."

"It's on speed dial," Kate said. "It's always been right before." She pressed the phone to her ear. The screaming continued. "Randi, if that's you, give me some kind of sign. Otherwise I'm going to call the police."

The screaming stopped. There was silence.

"Randi?" Kate said nervously. "Randi, are you still there?"

Nothing. Kate might have heard breathing, but she wasn't sure. "Randi?"

"Just give me a second," Randi said breathlessly.

Kate gave Teddy the thumbs-up. "Take your time," she said into the phone.

"Thanks," Randi gasped. "Sorry about the screaming . . . but I just saw something awful . . . I think I'm scarred for life . . . I'll probably have nightmares tonight."

"Did this awful thing have anything to do with what you saw on a certain webcam?" Kate asked.

"Oh, boy, did it ever!" Randi said.

"Get what you wanted?" Kate asked.

"Oh, yeah," Randi chuckled. "The fun has just begun. Give Teddy a big thank-you hug from me, okay?"

"Will do," Kate said, and hung up. "She said to give you a big thank-you hug."

"Any time," Teddy said.

"I say we save it for later," said Kate.

Teddy turned on the hot water in the cabana and they showered and changed. He offered to take her out to dinner, but Kate asked if they could stay there and grill on the deck. They had steak and salad and a bottle of red wine, and sat on the deck listening to the waves and watching the late-evening joggers and dog walkers.

Later, in the glow of a soft red-wine buzz, they took a blanket down to the beach. It seemed unusually dark, and at first Kate didn't understand why.

"It's a new moon," Teddy said. "Look at the stars."

Kate looked up. The stars were bright and glittering. Teddy

spread the blanket on the sand and they sat shoulder to shoulder and pulled their knees up under their chins.

"It's funny how fast the sand cools down at night, isn't it?" Kate said.

Teddy nodded.

"You think the porpoises are out there somewhere?" Kate asked.

"Don't know," Teddy said. "They're mammals, so you figure maybe they have to sleep, but who knows?"

"Guess we could look it up on the Internet," Kate said.

"Sounds like there'll be plenty of interesting stuff to look up on the Internet pretty soon," Teddy said. "Thanks to Randi."

"You mean, thanks to *you*," Kate said. "I really don't know how to thank you. You've done so much. You helped Randi, and Sonny Junior, and I've had such a wonderful time here."

"I do it because I can," Teddy said simply.

Kate kissed him on the cheek. It was meant to be a "thank you" kiss, but her lips stayed and kissed the side of his face again and again. Teddy turned and his lips met hers. They kissed for a while, and then Kate slowly lay back until her back touched the blanket. Teddy lay beside her, kissing and stroking her.

Kate gazed up at the sparkling night sky, cozy in Teddy's arms. That night last winter with Nick had been a mistake. She'd had too much to drink and had lost her head. Nick didn't count. Teddy was sweet and kind and good. She knew instinctively that he would never lie or cheat on her. As he slid his hand under her sweatshirt, Kate closed her eyes.

The next morning Kate slept late, then lay in bed, too comfortable to get up. The windows facing the beach were partly open and the sheer white curtains fluttered as the sea breeze came in. She could hear the steady crash of the waves on the sand. There was something about the steady growl of the surf and the cool fresh beach air that lent themselves to deep sleep.

Someone knocked lightly on her door. "Kate?"

It was Teddy.

"It's open. Come in," Kate said.

The door opened and she watched him come in. Kate couldn't help smiling as she remembered the night before, and what a wonderful, considerate lover Teddy had turned out to be. She was so lost in that memory that at first she didn't notice the stricken expression on his face.

And then she did. And at the same moment she realized he'd called her by her first name.

"Teddy, what is it?" she asked apprehensively.

He sat down on a corner of the bed and gave her a woeful look. Kate noticed a newspaper folded under his arm. Instead of answering, he reached toward her and gently stroked the hair off her forehead. "I just want you to know that nothing will change the way I feel about you."

Kate felt a shiver of dread. No one said that unless something so bad had happened that it very well *could* change the way he felt about her. Somehow she knew it had to do with the newspaper. She held out her hand.

Teddy handed her the paper. Halfway down on the right was a photo of her father, his hands cuffed behind him, being led from a car by two men in suits. The headline over the photo read:

FBI ARRESTS LOCAL MOBSTER
IN POLICE BRIBERY PROBE

Kate quickly skimmed the story. Not only had her father been arrested on charges of bribing the local police, but also for pirating DVDs and CDs and manufacturing knockoffs. The list of additional offenses seemed to go on forever: wire fraud, money laundering, tax evasion, racketeering, conspiracy.

Kate looked up at Teddy with tears in her eyes. "Oh, God, I'm sorry, Teddy. Really, I am."

"There's nothing to be sorry about," Teddy said, but as he said it, he looked away. It was the first time he hadn't been able to look her in the eye.

"Teddy?" Kate whispered.

He hung his head.

"Teddy, what is it?"

"My parents."

Kate felt an awful, sickening sensation. "They saw this?"

"My father's the one who found it," Teddy said.

Kate listened to the waves crashing. She felt the breeze come through the windows. Hot tears ran down her cheeks.

"Kate, listen," Teddy said. "This isn't my idea, but I have no choice. My parents . . . well, they're being real jerks. Only, this is their house and there's nothing I can do . . ."

She knew what he was going to say. She knew he didn't have the heart to say it himself.

"They want me to leave?" she asked.

Teddy nodded. "I'm so sorry, Kate. Really, I am."

WATCH YOUR BACK.

Count Your Blessings,

the final book in the Mob Princess trilogy,
is coming. . . .

IT WAS CLOSE TO EIGHT O'CLOCK WHEN KATE GOT HOME.
The sun was low in the west, sending long shadows across the
roads. A white van with the words DOMINIC'S POOL SERVICE on
the side was parked outside the driveway gate. *This has to be
some kind of mistake,* Kate thought as she drove up behind it.
They didn't use a pool service—her father had always insisted on
taking care of the pool himself. Kate suspected there was something therapeutic about it that relaxed him.

Kate pulled her car up behind the van and got out. In the van's
side-view mirror, Kate could see a guy with sunglasses sitting in
the front seat, watching her. She walked up to the window.

"I think there's some kind of mistake," she said.

"I don't think so."

Kate recognized the voice and blinked with astonishment.
"Nick?"

"I think you mean Dominic," Nick said with a funny accent. "Here to take care of your pool. What do you say you open the gate and let me in, okay?"

Kate was wary. What did he want? She tried to glance into the back of the truck.

"It's just me," Nick said, lowering his voice. "No tricks."

"What do you want?" Kate asked.

"Hey, I'm just trying to help you out here, lady," Nick said, still pretending to speak like some sort of New Yorker or something. "The boss says he owes you a favor."

It was true that Nick owed her a favor, but Kate still didn't know what to do. With her father in jail, this was the perfect time for the Blattarias to move in and take over once and for all. Meanwhile, the charade must have been for the benefit of any FBI guys hiding in the woods with shotgun microphones that could pick up conversations from a long way off.

"Look, I ain't got all day," Nick continued with the charade. "Like I said, I'm just trying to do you a favor. You ain't interested, I'll go." He leaned closer and whispered, "For Christ's sake, I'm risking my neck to be here, Kate."

He sounded sincere. Kate decided it was worth the risk. She went over to the keypad and opened the gate so that Nick could drive in. She followed him in her car. At the house, Nick got out of the truck wearing white pool-man uniform coveralls. It had been a while since Kate had seen him, and she'd forgotten those magnetic blue eyes and handsome face with that cleft chin. He was indeed handsome, but his looks did nothing for her at the moment. Right now, she was seriously missing Teddy.

He went around to the back of the truck and took out a white plastic bucket with some chemicals in it. Kate knew better than to question what he was doing. Instead she walked to the back of the house with him. Nick paused by the pool and looked around.

"Something I can help you with?" Kate asked.

"Where's your pool filter?" Nick asked.

This made no sense. They both knew Nick wasn't there to clean her pool.

"Nick, what's going on?" Kate asked.

Nick gave her a frustrated look. "Listen, lady, I'm Dominic. I don't know who Nick is. But if you don't show me that filter soon, I'm out of here."

Kate decided to play along, partly out of curiosity, and partly because he was already there so what did it matter? "It's back here," she said, leading him to the small pool house. Inside, it smelled of chlorine and the filter hummed. Kate waited while Nick put his hands on his hips and studied the filter. He reached down, adjusted a knob, and the pool house filled with a gurgling noise not unlike a washing machine.

"That should do it," Nick said in a low voice, barely audible over the sound of the filter.

"What'd you do?" Kate asked.

"I just increased the amount of air running through the system," Nick said. "It won't hurt anything." He looked around. "But it should make it noisy enough so that we can't be heard by any hidden mikes."

"My dad had this place thoroughly swept just a few weeks ago," Kate said.

"By Dee Bug?" Nick grinned.

Suddenly Kate felt a slightly nauseated. Obviously Nick knew something she didn't know. "They were FBI?" she asked.

Nick shook his head. "Our guys."

"*Your* guys?" Kate said. "That makes no sense. Why are we talking so quietly if they're your guys? Why do you care if they hear us?"

Nick pressed a finger to his lips. "Because I'm not here, okay?"

Kate didn't understand what game he was playing. But whatever it was, she wasn't interested. "What's going on? I mean it, Nick. Either you tell me right now or you can go."

"How are you?" Nick asked.

Kate rolled her eyes is disbelief. "I'm fine, thanks. How are you and Tiff?"

Nick's shoulders sagged. "Why do you always have to bring her up?"

"Oh, let's see . . ." Kate pressed her finger against her lips and gazed upward as if deep in thought. "I know! Maybe because you lied about not seeing her? Maybe because you were seeing her when you seduced me? Maybe because you were *still* seeing her when you pretended you were only seeing me?"

Nick stared at the floor and ran his fingers though his dark hair.

Kate found herself wishing he'd at least try to deny it. "Well?"

He raised his hands helplessly. "Look, that's what guys do."

Kate stared at him in disbelief as months worth of repressed anger boiled up inside her. "*That's* your best explanation? It's 'what guys do'? Well, let me tell you something, Mr. Casanova. That may be what guys do, but it's not what guys do *to me*. Understand? Now I've had enough of this crap. Either tell me why you're here, or get out."

"Okay, just try to keep it down, will you?" Nick said. "I came here to tell you I didn't know anything about the factory hit."

"Oh, give me a break," Kate said. "I am so tired of your lies." She turned to leave the pool house, but Nick grabbed her arm and tried to stop her. She angrily shook out of his grip. "Don't you ever touch me again. Do you understand?"

Nick grit his teeth. "Just listen. I didn't say we didn't do it. I said I didn't know about it."

Once again, Kate was confused. "Why tell me?"

"Because I want you to know, okay?" Nick said.

"Why? Why do you care?" Kate asked. "I don't get this, Nick. I really don't. You cheated on me. You lied to me. And now what is this? Can you give me the slightest reason why I should believe a word you say?"

Nick's face darkened. Kate had never seen him blush before. It was almost as if she were watching water come to a boil. "You know, you are just . . . !" he started to blurt, then caught himself.

"Just what?" Kate demanded. "Don't hold back, Nick. Or is it just so ingrained in your nature not to show your real feelings?"

"You . . . you . . ." Suddenly, he stepped closer, enveloped her in his arms, and pressed his lips against hers. Kate's mind went blank and her body was awash with emotion. This was wrong! So wrong! She was supposed to be kissing Teddy, not Nick! But something unexpected took hold of her. Something she'd thought she'd managed to get out of her system. But here it was, as strong as ever. She held him tight and kissed back with unexpected passion.

Was she out of her mind? After everything he'd done to her!?

What's life without a little . . .

DRAMA!

★ A new series by Paul Ruditis ★

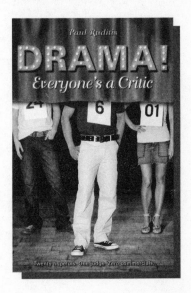

At Bryan Stark's posh private high school in Malibu, the teens are entitled, the boys are cute, and the school musicals are *extremely* elaborate. Bryan watches—and comments—as the action and intrigue unfold around him. Thrilling mysteries, comic relief, and epic sagas of friendship and love . . . It's all here. And it's showtime.

From Simon Pulse • Published by Simon & Schuster